AUGUSTUS HELPS THE ARMY

Le Grand has also written:

AUGUSTUS AND THE RIVER
AUGUSTUS GOES SOUTH
AUGUSTUS AND THE MOUNTAINS
AUGUSTUS HELPS THE NAVY

AUGUSTUS
HELPS THE ARMY

by

LE GRAND

THE BOBBS-MERRILL COMPANY

INDIANAPOLIS   NEW YORK

THE CORNWALL PRESS, INC., CORNWALL, N.Y.

AUGUSTUS HELPS THE ARMY

CHAPTER ONE

Augustus untied his shoelaces and slipped his feet out of his shoes. That felt better and he wiggled his freed toes happily as he leaned back against the softly cushioned seat and looked around the big bus. Outside, the pine trees and white farmhouses of New England flashed past the windows.

Augustus had never been on a bus before. He bounced a little in his seat, just to prove to himself that the cushions were as soft as he thought they were.

"Georgia," he said aloud. "Goin' all the way to Georgia on these good ol' cushions."

He glanced sideways at the soldier who sat in the seat beside him. The soldier wore a corporal's stripes on his sleeve. Augustus wanted to talk to him. But the corporal was reading a magazine. Augustus looked around for some way of getting his attention.

In the seat ahead, Augustus' small brother Jupiter and his sister Glorianna turned their heads from side to side as they tried to see everything at once. Like Augustus, Jupiter and Glorianna had never been in a bus before. And neither had Pop and Ma, who sat two or three seats ahead of Jupiter and Glorianna and on the other side of the bus. Pop sat very stiff and straight and didn't seem to be comfortable. He wore a high stiff collar and a necktie. That had been Ma's idea. She had given Augustus a quarter to go down to the store and buy the necktie for Pop. Augustus was proud of his selection. It had more colors in it than any other necktie on the bus. Augustus thought Pop looked very nice except that the collar seemed to bother him and he kept running his finger around the edge of it.

The window beside Glorianna was open a little and her hair blew over the back of her seat. That gave Augustus the idea he needed to get the corporal's attention. Lifting his bare foot suddenly, he caught Glorianna's hair between his toes and pulled. Augustus' toes were very useful that way. He had spent a lot of time training them until he could pick up stones and things almost as well with his feet as with his hands.

Glorianna squawked so loudly that everyone on the bus turned to see what was going on. Augustus made sure the corporal was watching him and then yanked again.

But now a new sound rose over Glorianna's angry protests. It was Ma's voice. "You, Augustus!"

Augustus let go of Glorianna's hair, but his heel was hooked over the back of her seat and he couldn't get it down. Ma's eyes fastened on his bare, wiggling toes, and Augustus suddenly remembered her stern warning not to take his shoes off on the bus.

"I declare to the everlasting mountains!" said Ma.

"What will folks think of us, with you a-ridin' barefoot right on the bus? I told you it wasn't polite."

Ma got up and started down the aisle toward Augustus. The bus was bouncing over a rough stretch of road and Ma swayed from side to side. Augustus got his foot down at last, grabbed his shoes and tried to get his feet into them. Ma was advancing steadily when the bus driver saw her in his rear-vision mirror.

"Now, lady," the driver said, "you'll have to sit down in the bus. First thing you know, we'll be swinging round a curve and you'll get thrown through the air like a dickey bird."

The idea of Ma's stout figure flying through the air like a dickey bird brought a grin to the faces of the other passengers. Ma thought it was funny herself. She never could stay angry very long.

"Well, I do declare," she gasped and began to laugh as she went back to her seat.

The other passengers laughed with her and Pop said, "Now looka there, Ma, it's just like I told you, these folks are just folks an' I'm a-goin' to take off this blame collar. Why, fry me for a catfish, the thing's a-scrapin' my neck as raw as a skinned eel." Pop took the collar off and sighed happily.

Ma hesitated a little and then she unbuttoned her coat which was rather tight. "Well," she said, "it *is* a great comfort to a body to be comfortable."

Augustus decided that maybe it wouldn't be necessary

for him to put his shoes on now and he waggled his toes as he beamed brightly at the corporal, who smiled back at him and said, "Where you folks going, boy?"

Augustus was glad he could say proudly, "Oh, we're goin' to help the Army down in Georgia."

The soldier said, "Oh?"

Augustus was squirming to tell his story and his words came out like a burst of machine-gun fire. "Yeh, you see first we lived out on the Mississippi River, in a houseboat, an' then we went way up in the mountains in Kentucky an' then we heard about the war an' then Pop he fixed up his ol' car and we went to Maine so's Pop could work in a shipyard and help out with the war, but then Pop found out that they weren't makin' ships out of wood, an' Pop didn't know how to make ships out of iron and steel an' stuff like that, an' then Pop heard about how they needed men that could work with wood to make a big Army camp down in Georgia."

Augustus paused for a quick breath and when he went on he was grinning a little. "An' I guess Pop he kind of liked the idea of goin' south for the winter anyway. Pop always says that the winters in the North bring on a sort of epidemic in his back."

Augustus rubbed his back to show where the Northern winters hurt Pop. "An' besides, it was gettin' on to be time for the ducks to fly south an' Pop he can't hardly stand to see the ducks fly south without goin' along too."

Augustus gulped in another breath. "But our tires were mighty no 'count an' we couldn't get enough gas but Pop he saved a little money from workin' at the shipyard an' from sellin' what was left of the car, so we up an' decided to come on a bus an' so here we are an' I never rode on a bus before but I like it fine."

The corporal seemed a little bewildered by such a rush of words in such a short time. He blinked at Augustus and said, "Oh, and are you going to help the Army too?"

Augustus' answer came immediately and with no hesitation. "Yeh, sure, I betcha a thousand million dollars I will."

He looked so determined and confident that the soldier said, "Well, I don't happen to have a thousand million dollars with me right now—must have left it in my other uniform—but I'd be afraid to bet if I did have it because I expect you probably *will* help out somehow or other."

Augustus and the corporal talked as the bus sped on. Augustus learned that the soldier's name was Griggs and that he was in a tank brigade. Corporal Griggs was careful not to say anything that should not be said, but he told enough about the Army to make Augustus glad and proud that it was *his* Army. And Augustus was more determined than ever to do something to help.

But as the sun went down and it grew dark in the bus, both Corporal Griggs and Augustus began to yawn. Augustus saw some of the other passengers tilt their seats back and fall asleep. Augustus found and pulled the lever that let his seat tilt back. He stretched out and watched the stars twinkle and the moon rise. The movement of the bus was soothing. Augustus was asleep.

He woke to find the moon high in the sky. The bus had stopped. The driver stood by the door and he was saying something that sounded like, "Wahblah, North Carolina. This is a five-minute rest stop, folks."

The passengers that were awake got up and shuffled out of the bus. Augustus and Corporal Griggs went out too. The bus had stopped beside a small gas station and lunchroom which was a tiny spot of glaring lights in the midst of the great darkness of the night. Tall trees hung over three or four small unlighted buildings. And that, as far as Augustus could see, was all there was of the town that sounded like "Wahblah, North Carolina."

Another big bus came in and stopped and more sleepy people stumbled out into the lights from the lunchroom. It gave Augustus a curious feeling to be standing there in the darkness, not knowing what or where the place was, and to watch the people from the two buses who didn't know one another or where they were either. Here they had all met and in five minutes the two buses would go off in opposite directions and probably none of them would ever see the village of "Wahblah, North Carolina," again, or ever learn what its name really was.

Augustus went into the lunchroom with Corporal Griggs. The corporal learned that the lunchroom was a post office too, and he started to write a postal card. Augustus had a nickel and he went to the little lunch counter where people were crowded two deep. Augustus was thirsty and he saw a sign on the wall advertising strawberry soda. He tried to squeeze through the crowd but couldn't make it. He scratched his ear for a minute and then dropped to his hands and knees. Crawling between the legs of the men in front of him, he popped up under the nose of the startled man nearest the counter. He got his soda. It was pink, and cold, and wet. Augustus let it trickle down his throat slowly as he squeezed away from the counter.

Corporal Griggs had finished his postal card and mailed it. Augustus saw him hesitate and then stand patiently waiting for a chance to get to the lunch counter. The driver of Augustus' bus came to the door and shouted that the five minutes were nearly up. The men in front of Corporal Griggs got what they wanted and came away. The corporal said, "Ham sandwich, please." But before he could get to the counter a woman from the second bus swooped in from the side and squeezed in ahead of him. The corporal blinked and Augustus scowled. The woman was big. She had a loud voice. She looked as if she were angry at everyone and everything and had always been that way. She said she wanted a ham sandwich. When it came she said, "Huh, I want rye bread and this is white—take it away."

The counterman said, "I don't have any rye bread, lady."

She snorted, "Then give me whole-wheat bread."

The counterman sighed softly and said, "But I don't have any whole-wheat bread."

Corporal Griggs shifted from one foot to another and tried to get the counterman's attention.

The bus driver shouted, "Time's up—all aboard."

The large angry woman snapped, "Well, leave the sandwich here—maybe I'll eat it later, but give me some tomato soup first."

Corporal Griggs looked at the counterman who was going off to get the soup. He looked over his shoulder toward the bus. The driver started the motor and blew his horn. The corporal started to turn away sadly. But Augustus had seen something on the wall beside him. It was a large black spider slowly lowering itself on a long silky thread. Augustus reached up, wound the thread around his finger and with the spider dangling about a foot below his hand, he squeezed between the corporal and the woman. She was sitting on a stool. Augustus reached over her head. The spider lowered away until he was opposite the woman's nose. He apparently decided that would be a good solid place to attach his web and started to do so. Then things happened fast. A loud *"Yowp!"* screeched through the little lunchroom. Augustus was knocked over backward and two large feet scrambled over him and out the door. Augustus didn't have much breath left in him but he jumped up and shouted to Corporal Griggs, "Take the sandwich—that was what you wanted!"

The corporal grabbed the sandwich, dropped some money on the counter and dashed out the door after Augustus. The bus was already moving but the driver saw them and opened the door. He shook his head. "Just one more second and you'd have been left."

Augustus and Corporal Griggs dropped into their seats.

The corporal munched his sandwich. He turned and grinned at Augustus, "Boy," he said, "you were saying you wanted to help the Army. Well, you've done it!"

Augustus grinned back. "Oh, yeh," he said happily. "But you just wait, I'm going to do more than that."

The corporal nodded. "I believe you," he said.

Chapter Two

A more intense sunlight than that of Maine glared on a rolling countryside that was startlingly new to Augustus. The grass and trees were the usual green but the earth was a bright brick-red. This, with the brilliant blue sky, gave Augustus the feeling that he had stepped from the bus into a new and more colorful world.

It was the third day since he had left Maine. Corporal Griggs had got off the bus late the night before and since then Augustus had been more and more anxious to get to Fort Lee and to see what his new home was like.

And now he was there. Pop carried the last of their suitcases and bundles from the bus and said, "Well, here we are, folks. I got you to Blytheville, Georgia, just like I said I would."

His yellow mustache lifted in a broad grin and he slapped Ma playfully on the back. Pop's hand was big and heavy and his playfulness knocked Ma's breath out.

"Huh!" she snorted. "Precious little you had to do with getting us here." She turned and smiled pleasantly at the driver. "This young man is who got us here," she announced.

The driver waved his hand in a friendly manner and started his motor.

"Wait! wait!" Ma shouted. "Land sakes, I want to thank you."

The bus door was still open and Ma clambered aboard. Grabbing the surprised driver's hand, she shook it vigorously.

"Young man," she said, "last night I got to worryin' about you when it turned a mite cool an' you up here a-drivin' with land knows how many drafts a-blowin' on you."

The driver blinked. "Oh, that's all right, lady," he said. "I ——"

Ma broke in. "'Tis not all right an' I stayed awake nearly all night to fix it for you." Ma's expression was triumphant as she groped in her bag and pulled something out. "Here," she said. "A nice red flannel throat-warmer that I made myself. I declare, it's lucky I had that piece of flannel in my bag."

Before the startled driver knew what Ma intended to do, she had slipped the piece of cloth around his throat and was tying it in the back.

"There now," Ma said, "that'll be a comfort to you, I'm sure." She shook hands again and stepped off the bus. "Good-by," she called. "Have a nice trip."

Pop and Augustus and Glorianna and Jupiter waved to the driver and shouted, "Good-by!"

The driver caught a glimpse of himself in the rear-vision mirror. He also saw the faces of the passengers and his own face grew as red as the flannel that glowed brightly around his throat. "G-g-by," he said in a curious voice and the motor roared as the bus started with a jerk and was gone down the long highway where the heat waves rose and shimmered.

Pop coughed a little. "Kind of a hot day for a throat-warmer," he said.

"Well, maybe," said Ma, "but likely it'll turn cool come nightfall."

When the bus had disappeared, Augustus turned his attention to the town of Blytheville, weighing in his mind the chances for excitement there. It was a typical Southern small town. A block of stores faced the highway and there were two cross streets where houses clustered thickly at first and then grew farther and farther apart as the streets meandered off toward fields of cotton and wooded hills.

In front of the stores a wooden canopy projected over the sidewalk, providing a shade that felt good even though it was late September and the weather had been cool when Augustus left Maine.

However, it was more than the heat that made Blytheville a typically Southern town. Two comfortably drowsy hound-dogs sprawled happily in the middle of the road, secure in the knowledge that all car drivers would considerately avoid them.

At least half the people in sight were Negroes and both

white and colored folk seemed to have time to stand in the shade and talk and laugh with their friends.

Augustus decided he would like Blytheville, but he had something else on his mind. "Where's the camp, Pop?" he asked.

"Well now, I reckon it's out of town a piece," Pop answered. "Most likely it's off where there's enough room for a passel of soldiers to move around without bumpin' into other folks."

Pop looked at the pile of suitcases and bundles at his feet and his expression grew thoughtful. He rubbed his back and grunted a little.

"Reckon we'll just leave those things there for a spell," he said and rubbed his back again. "I can feel that ol' epidemic in my back a-startin' again an' I wouldn't want to strain it any a-totin' too many things right away. After all the South hasn't hardly had time to limber my back up yet."

Ma narrowed her eyes at him. She opened her mouth to say something and Pop looked around a little wildly.

Suddenly his expression brightened. He pointed to a small bus coming up one of the side streets. A sign on it said "Camp Lee." The "epidemic" in Pop's back apparently didn't interfere with his running as he dashed toward the bus, shouting to Ma, "Goin' out to the camp to see about gettin' work—you find us a place to live. I'll be back before night an' meet you right here."

Ma grumbled a little. Then she said, "Well, I reckon you young'uns 'll just have to stay here with our belongin's whilst I hunt up a place to live. Now mind you don't go off or get into any trouble." She went up the street.

Augustus sat on one of the bundles and looked around. These first few hours in a new place always interested Augustus. He liked the sense of strangeness, of seeing new and different things.

He was fascinated by the redness of these roads and fields and hills. This was a country of hills, big ones and little ones, high ones and low ones, and all were red beneath their green foliage.

Augustus watched the people and listened to them talk. He found so many things to look at and wonder about that he didn't realize how long he had been sitting there until Jupiter said, "I guess it must be dinnertime, I guess, huh?"

Augustus started to say, "Aw, always thinkin' about your stummick," but then he decided that he was hungry too. Pop and Ma had been gone for hours.

Glorianna opened the box of food. She said, "There's some biscuits left—an' mmmm! here's some cooked hamburgers." She held the meat up and looked at it. "Be a lot better hot," she said.

Augustus said, "Aw," just because he always disagreed with Glorianna, but he didn't say it as scornfully as usual.

They had been eating cold food from the box ever since they left Maine. Augustus pulled his left ear thoughtfully and looked around. They were in front of the block of stores that made up the town's business section. There were several parked cars at the curb and other cars passed frequently in the street. Augustus decided that maybe this was not exactly the right place to build a campfire. A little farther down the street he saw a vacant lot between two stores.

"Come on," he said and picked up the box of food. "You find the frying pan," he told Glorianna.

The vacant lot was littered with old boards and Augustus soon had a fire going.

Before this, people passing by to shop in the stores had looked at the little group beside the pile of baggage, and then gone on. But when the fire was going nicely and the meat sizzled in the pan, Augustus found a small crowd had gathered on the sidewalk in front of the vacant lot, watching him interestedly.

Augustus gazed back at them with equal interest. He thought it was friendly of them to notice him and he wished he had enough lunch to invite them all to have some.

"Well, I never!" said an old lady, her voice shrill with astonishment. A younger woman giggled.

A man came up to the fire and drawled, "What you kids think you're doing?"

Augustus considered that a silly question but he said reasonably, "Why, we're just cookin' our dinner."

The corners of the man's mouth twitched upward. He had a pleasant face. "And do you always cook your dinner on a campfire right in the middle of town?" he asked.

By this time the old lady had come up to the fire. She tried to fan the smoke away from her face as she peered near-sightedly into the frying pan. "Well, I never!" she said again.

"It's true—for a while I thought my eyes were fooling me. You know they're not so good as they once were."

She bent over to look at Jupiter, who seemed to think she was after his hamburger. He grabbed it from the pan, slapped it on a biscuit and retreated, chewing furiously.

The old lady said, "Well, I never! Mr. Beverley, who are these children?"

The pleasant-faced man said, "Why, Miss Emma Lu, I don't know. Who are you, boy?" he asked Augustus. "Where are you-all's folks?"

Augustus explained, fixing himself a hamburger and gnawing it between sentences.

Mr. Beverley said, "I expect your father won't have any trouble getting work at the camp; they need all the men they can get out there." He went on seriously, "But I'm not so sure your mother will find a house. So many people have come here to work at the camp that there just aren't enough houses in town to go around."

Augustus said proudly, "Oh, that's all right, we came down here to help the Army and I betcha we won't let any ol' house stop us." He snorted, "Shucks, we hardly ever lived in a house anyway."

Old Miss Emma Lu gasped and Mr. Beverley looked puzzled until Augustus told him how they had lived in a houseboat on the Mississippi River and in a schooner on the Maine coast. "Why, the only time we lived in a house was when we went to see Uncle Lem up in the Kentucky mountains. Uncle Lem's house was made of logs."

Mr. Beverley seemed impressed. "My, my," he said. "You've traveled around nearly as much as those circus people who were here last week."

"Circus?" shouted Jupiter joyously.

"Yes," said Mr. Beverley, "but it's gone now." He shook his head sadly. "They ran out of money and had to leave some of their things here to pay their bills. I got one of their tents for their grocery bill at my store. Don't know what I'll ever do with the thing but ——"

Mr. Beverley was interrupted by a shout from the street. "Augustus, Glorianna, Jupiter, where are you? Where's your Ma? Where's anybody? Why, chop me up for a fish chowder, this here is a fine way to greet a man that's just got him a job with the guv'ment a-buildin' camps for soldiers."

"There's Pop," Augustus said happily. "Hey, Pop, here we are!"

Chapter Three

Pop's grin stretched clear across his face as he strode past the group of people and up to Augustus. "Yessirree," he bellowed. "Your Pop's a-workin' for the guv'ment now. Always knew Uncle Sam would know a good man when he saw him."

Pop was so pleased with himself that Mr. Beverley and the other people in the group were pleased too—even to old Miss Emma Lu, who said, "Well, I never!" and then laughed.

"What about a house to live in?" asked Mr. Beverley.

"Oh, Ma will take care of that," answered Pop easily. "I always say, just set Ma to trackin' something down and you've as good as got it."

Mr. Beverley looked a little doubtful. He was still looking that way when Ma appeared, breathing heavily as she pushed past the others and up to Pop.

"Land sakes!" panted Ma. "I do declare I never had such a time in all my born days." She sat down, took her shoes off and rubbed her feet tenderly. "I do declare to the everlasting mountains," she sighed, "I've been all over this town an' I mighty nigh didn't get a thing to live in."

"But you did find something?" Pop asked hopefully.

"Well, yes an' no," was Ma's answer. "I found a house and a right nice house it would be too—if it only had a roof on it."

"No—roof?" said Pop.

"No roof," said Ma. "I figure you can put a roof on it in your spare time, an' the man that owns it says he'll take your work for the rent so that's all right." She stopped and looked at the sky. "Only trouble is, it might set to rainin' before you get it covered."

Mr. Beverley gazed at the sky. Miss Emma Lu gazed at the sky. Quite a crowd had collected by this time and everyone gazed at the sky.

"Th' almanac says rain," announced a lean, tanned farmer.

"Mm," said Pop and scratched his head slowly.

Mr. Beverley scratched his head. Old Miss Emma Lu scratched her head and then, realizing what she was doing, suddenly stopped and turned red. "Well, I never!" she gasped.

Everyone was quiet and Augustus' shout sounded very loud. "I know," he bellowed. "Mr. Beverley's tent—he could let us have it until we can get that roof fixed."

"Tent?" asked Ma.

Mr. Beverley blinked. "Why, so I could," he said. Turning to Ma he went on, "Yes, ma'am, if you wouldn't mind living in a tent you can have it and welcome." He smiled. "Of course there's a good many of you but this is a circus tent and pretty big—not the main tent of course, but it's still pretty big."

Pop slapped Mr. Beverley's back happily. "Why, cut me up for fish bait," he said, "that's mighty nice of you. Real Southern hospitality I'd call it. Mighty fine folks in Georgia. I'd purely like to live in a tent." Pop looked up at the sky and chuckled. "Now come on an' rain," he whooped. "Rain on the roof of a tent is one of the prettiest sounds I know— haven't heard it since I was a boy."

Mr. Beverley's grocery truck was soon loaded with the tent, Pop, Ma, Augustus, Glorianna, Jupiter, their baggage and a colored boy named Abraham who drove the truck and would help pitch the tent. Abraham drove out a side street and kept going until all the houses of the town were behind.

They went another half-mile and then as the truck swung around a wide curve Ma said, "There it is over yonder."

The house was a very old one. It was made of squared logs and the big old chimney was built of stones. Abraham said he reckoned it was about the oldest house thereabouts and probably one of the first to be built in that part of Georgia. It stood on a low wooded hill that overlooked a wide sweep of fields and valleys. A few fruit trees gone wild showed above the high weeds in back and a few wild rose bushes in front disclosed that once a flower garden had been there.

On one side an open pasture facing the road seemed to

be the best place for the tent. Because it was so big, the tent was heavy and hard to raise. When it was up and securely staked everybody was puffing and panting.

"There she is," said Pop, "an' if I do say so myself, she's a beauty—erk!"

The queer sound Pop made at the end came when he raised his eyes and saw what was beside the tent's entrance. Everyone had been too busy to notice it before. The noise Pop made was nothing compared with Ma's sudden bellow when she saw what Pop was looking at. Ma's eyes popped and her whole body was frozen in an attitude of outraged protest. On one side of the entrance was a big picture of an unbelievably fat woman whose enormous cheeks were curved in a huge smile as she looked across the entrance at the sign on the other side. The sign said: SEE SALLY THE FAT LADY——10¢

"I won't live in it," Ma shouted furiously. "The idea! Why—why——" Ma stopped as she realized that there was a stranger standing in the road staring at her.

It was a red-haired boy about Augustus' size. He continued to stare at Ma as he went up to Augustus and said, "Is she the one?"

"Is who what one?" Augustus asked.

"Why, the one on the sign," the boy said. "Sally—the Fat Lady."

Ma's face turned purple. "That settles it," she announced. "I won't live in it an' that's that." She ducked into the tent to get out of sight of any other people who might come by.

"Shucks," said the red-haired boy. "She's not so fat. Why, I betcha my sister is fatter than she is."

Augustus scowled. "Look," he said. "That's no Sally the Fat Lady, that's my Ma, an' you better be careful what you say around here."

The boy shook his head bewilderedly. "I didn't mean anything wrong," he said. "I'm Jaybird Hardy an' I live up the road there. I was going home an' I saw the sign an' the lady. Well, if she doesn't want folks to think she's fat why does she put up a big sign tellin' 'em she is?"

He said this so reasonably that Augustus' scowl vanished, helped also by Pop's attitude. Pop was sitting on the ground and rocking back and forth. He had both hands clasped tightly over his mouth but, even so, choked howls of laughter broke through.

"Oh, oh," he spluttered. "Haven't had as much fun since the time the snake scared Ma an' she sat on the hot stove." Tears dribbled down Pop's cheeks.

"Oh, is that so?" Ma snapped, her flushed face appearing in the entrance. "Well, you can have some more fun taking this tent down right away. I just wouldn't stay in the thing for love or money."

Pop began to look a little concerned. "Aw now, Ma," he began, but Ma had disappeared again.

Pop turned to Augustus. "This here is beginning to look serious," he said. "I believe your Ma means it."

Jaybird was looking so confused that Augustus explained to him how they came to have Sally, the Fat Lady's tent.

Jaybird said, "Well, dog my cats, no wonder your Ma is mad—if she didn't know about that sign before."

"Yeh," said Augustus. "Well, I guess I'll have to do something about it."

Jaybird made the kind of noise that indicated he was willing to be helpful but didn't know how to begin.

Augustus pulled his left ear thoughtfully and then the right one. He puffed out his cheeks and whistled a long sour note. He stared at the tent.

"It's Mr. Beverley's tent," he thought. "Maybe he'd know what to do." It was when he thought of Mr. Beverley that the idea came to him. "I know," he said. "That sign in Mr. Beverley's grocery store—that'll fix it." He turned to Jaybird. "Do you have any paint at your house?"

Jaybird nodded. "Pa usually has some."

"Well, I need it," Augustus said earnestly. "Can I borrow some?"

"Sure, come on." Jaybird led the way up the road.

When they came back, Augustus had a can of paint and a brush. Ma was collecting her belongings and announcing she was moving over to the roofless house, rain or no rain. Augustus walked up to the sign on the tent and dipped his brush into the paint. He crossed out the words "See" and "Sally" and printed "Save" instead. Then he crossed out "Lady" and wrote "And Win the War." With a satisfied expression he stepped back and cocked his head as he examined his work. The sign now read: SAVE THE FAT AND WIN THE WAR.

"Guess that'll do," Augustus said. "Hey, Ma—look."

Ma looked. She blinked and looked again. "Why, I do declare," she said slowly. "Why, I do declare to the hills and the treetops. Why, that's real nice—an' it's so patriotic and all." Ma began to chuckle. "I'll be purely proud to live here now," she said. "And what's more, I'll save every bit of cooking fat I can and bring it to Mr. Beverley's store so he can send it off to where they make gunpowder for the Army."

Chapter Four

Augustus and Jaybird found they had similar ideas on a great many things. Jaybird lived on a farm but he liked roaming in the woods better than farm work. Augustus felt that way too.

Neither of them liked to wear shoes. "Blame ol' things," Augustus said. "If you wore things like that over your face you couldn't breathe an' you'd die. Well, I guess your feet have some rights too, don't they?"

"Reckon so." Jaybird decided to remember that argument for future use.

Augustus didn't like to comb his hair and neither did Jaybird. A tuft of Jaybird's hair always rose up from the top of his head and looked like a jaybird's crest. That was how he got his name.

The one thing Augustus and Jaybird were most completely agreed upon was admiration for the Army. When the work of getting settled in the tent was over, Augustus asked Pop if he and Jaybird could go through the camp. Pop said he would try to get them a pass.

When Pop went off to work, promising that he wouldn't forget about the pass, Augustus started out to find Jaybird.

He found him at home and looking rather glum.

Augustus said, "Hey!"

Jaybird said, "Huh!"

Augustus considered Jaybird's unhappy expression and said, "What's the matter?"

Jaybird looked sourly at the sky. "It looks like rain," he said, "an' I have to help pick the last of the cotton crop because the rain would spoil it."

Augustus made sympathetic noises.

Jaybird wrinkled his nose and said, "My father can't get any field hands to help him—they've all gone off to do war work."

Jaybird's father heard that as he came out of the house. "Yes," he said, "and that would be all right except that raising cotton is war work too—and mighty important war work. Why, the government needs cotton for all kinds of war industries."

Jaybird's father believed in the importance of cotton. He had spent all his life raising it. His sun-browned face grew enthusiastic as he continued to talk about how necessary it was in the war effort. Augustus listened. He was impressed.

Jaybird's father said, "Why, picking cotton is nearly as important right now as being a soldier."

Augustus hadn't thought of it in that way before. If cotton picking was like being a soldier it must be pretty exciting, he decided. And if it would be helping out with the war . . . Augustus seemed to see himself in the middle of a cotton field pulling furiously at great fuzzy clumps of cotton while

Uncle Sam and the President and all the members of Congress stood around him applauding loudly.

He looked at Jaybird's father with determination in his eye. "Mr. Hardy," he said, "I'll do it. I'll help pick the cotton."

Jaybird's expression brightened. He felt that working in the fields would be much more interesting with Augustus helping.

Augustus was alight with enthusiasm now. "And I'll get Glorianna and Jupiter to help too," he said. " 'Course Glorianna's only a girl but she's pretty good sometimes. Jupiter—well, he's kind of small but I expect he can help all right for his size."

Jaybird and his father were both pleased. Augustus arranged to meet them in the cotton field and then went to find Glorianna and Jupiter.

They were in the woods back of the tent. Jupiter was happily making imitation hamburgers out of mud, while Glorianna baked them in the ashes of a small fire.

"Aw," said Augustus. "Stop thinkin' of your stummick for a minute, can't you?"

Jupiter looked mildly surprised. He didn't see why anyone would want to think of anything else.

When Augustus explained about the cotton picking and how it would be helping the country, Glorianna said, "Why, it'll be just like being a WAAC. Sure, I'll come."

Jupiter decided that making mud hamburgers all by himself wouldn't be much fun and he agreed to go too.

Glorianna whispered to Augustus, "I'm glad he's coming. I'd be afraid to leave him here alone—why, he gets to thinking those things are real and he might eat some!"

The wide cotton fields back of Jaybird's house had nearly all been stripped of their crop. Only one small field glowed white against the red earth and green leaves.

"We had some field hands for most of the crop," Jaybird explained, "but the last one left before they got to this patch."

Mr. Hardy said, "I'll pay you boys—" he looked again at Glorianna—"and the young lady fifty cents for every hundred pounds you pick. That's the regular rate. Here's a bag for each of you. Now go to it, and we'd better get it all in before that rain comes up."

Glorianna seemed somewhat startled. She had never been called "young lady" before. It made her feel very grown up and very different from the boys. She wasn't sure she liked to feel that way.

"All right, 'young lady,'" Augustus grunted, "stir your stumps. Didn't you hear him say we have to hurry?"

Glorianna grinned and felt more natural. She picked up a bag, hung it over her shoulder and followed Augustus into the long, white rows of cotton.

Jupiter said, "Mm, we get paid. Mmm, money! Mmm, I'll go down to the store and get some candy." He started to pick cotton but Augustus heard him still mumbling,

"Pickles, an' maybe a pie, maybe, an' some ice cream, I guess. Oh boy!"

Augustus started off with a rush and was well down his row while the others were still getting their bags properly hung over their shoulders and settling down to their jobs.

To Augustus, every cotton bush was a Jap or a German. "I'll show you," he muttered fiercely. Grabbing the fluffy cotton fibers he jerked them away from the bolls that held them. "There, I guess that'll fix you. Oh, so you won't surrender, huh? Well, how do you like that? I guess maybe you don't think you're so smart now, do you?" That much conversation usually took care of one plant. Then to another one, "Oh, so *you're* goin' to get fresh now, are you? Well, take that—an' that."

He shuffled down the row with his arms flying. The sun blazed down on the open field. Red dust rose under the shuffling feet. Augustus' back felt damp. Trickles of sweat rolled down his neck. The dust settled there. It stuck and dried. At first it tickled and then it became uncomfortable, irritating.

Flies and gnats buzzed around Augustus' head. They crawled on his bare arms and neck. The gnats showed an insane desire to drown themselves in his eyes. Some of them succeeded.

The cotton plants began to look less and less like enemy soldiers. The whole business of cotton picking began to feel like hard work. Augustus slowed down. Jaybird's father was

ahead of him now. Augustus didn't mind that. He didn't
really expect to keep up with him. Jaybird worked up until
he was even with him. Augustus didn't mind that either.

Then he saw that Glorianna had nearly caught up with

him. That was different. Augustus worked faster again. He drew ahead of Glorianna. But she worked steadily and when Augustus slowed down again, she was nearly even with him.

They went up and down the long rows and now the competition with Glorianna was the force that drove Augustus to keep up his pace.

When the sacks were full, Augustus enjoyed the rest while Mr. Hardy weighed them at the scales he carried in the mule-drawn wagon that followed the pickers through the field.

Glorianna's sack held nearly as much cotton as Augustus' and she had picked it nearly as fast.

"Fine," said Mr. Hardy. "We'll have this patch picked clean in no time. Just keep it up and this cotton will be safe in my barn before the rain comes." He smiled at Glorianna. "You're doing as well as the boys," he said. Glorianna strutted happily back to her row.

"Just wait," Augustus said, "I'll show you on the next sack." The cotton plants were no longer the enemy. Glorianna had taken on that place.

Augustus pushed on through the heat and the flies and the gnats. It was a very annoying kind of competition to him, because although he was stronger than Glorianna, there was no way to make his strength count. Glorianna could pick a tuft of cotton as easily as he could. Besides, she was steadier. Augustus liked to do things with a sudden explosion of effort and then rest a while. Glorianna didn't seem to mind plodding along for hours at the same steady monotonous pace.

When the second bags were weighed, the result was about the same as before. Glorianna had picked nearly as much and almost as fast as Augustus had.

There was about enough left to pick to make one more sackful for everyone and a little left over for Jupiter who straggled around the field picking a few of the biggest and fluffiest bolls.

"This time I'll show her," Augustus grunted, and he swung into action like a small tornado. He was way ahead of Glorianna when he bumped into Jupiter who was standing still and looking at something in the next field. "What you doin', just standin' there gawkin'?" Augustus asked.

Jupiter pointed to some vines growing in the other field. "Sweet potatoes," he announced. "We could dig 'em up an' bake 'em— Mmm, good!"

Jaybird's father was working near by and he looked up and smiled. "You like sweet potatoes, boy?" he asked.

Jupiter's answer was a loud and expressive, "Mmm-mm," accompanied by a vigorous rubbing of his stomach.

"Well, they're ripe now; dig yourself a few and take them home with you."

Jupiter gazed gratefully at this man who had such good ideas.

"How many can I have?" he asked.

"Jupiter!" Augustus scowled at his small brother, distressed by his greediness.

But Jupiter was not interested in manners; he was interested in sweet potatoes. He repeated his question. "How many can I have?"

Jaybird's father laughed. "As many as you can tote off," he said. "I guess that won't be more than I can afford to lose."

Jupiter found a pointed stick and went to work grabbling for potatoes.

When Augustus came back that way as he worked up the next row, he saw Jupiter still digging.

Glorianna was far behind and Augustus' bag was much fuller than hers, so he stopped for a minute to see how Jupiter was coming on.

A slight scurrying at his feet caught his attention and he looked down to see a big black ant being carried off by two smaller but apparently fiercer ants who were part red and part black.

As Augustus watched he saw two more red and black ants carrying off another black one. Then he saw other small but violent struggles all around him.

"Why, it's a regular battle," he thought, and bent over to watch the warfare more closely.

It seemed to be an organized raid by the red and black ants on a nest belonging to the all-black ones. A long line of the attackers rushed up to the entrance holes of the blacks' nest and swarmed in. They came out in pairs and every combat team of two carried a struggling black between them.

Sometimes an especially big, strong black beat off his enemies and sometimes even killed them. But even these champions were finally carried off and killed by the tigerish little red and black ants.

The battle was practically over when Augustus remem-

bered his cotton picking. To his dismay he saw that Glorianna had passed him and nearly finished her rows. Her sack
bulged. Augustus looked at his. He was pleased to see that it
was fuller than he had thought. Still Glorianna had more and
she was nearer finished.

This was the kind of situation that stirred Augustus to
a real effort. He rushed back to the field and picked cotton so
fast that it seemed to be jumping from the plants into his sack.

He gained on Glorianna. She was tired and although
she was still picking steadily she was not going very fast.

Augustus' tremendous rush carried him on but Glorianna had reached the end of the rows assigned to her when
Augustus caught up.

Glorianna's sack was full and she had finished just a
shade ahead of Augustus. But Augustus was not beaten yet.
For some time he had noticed that his sack was heavier than
it had ever been before. He was sure Glorianna's sack didn't
hold as much cotton.

"She wouldn't be toting it around easy as that if it was
as heavy as mine," he told himself hopefully.

On the way to the scales, Augustus realized that he was
about worn out from carrying the heavy sack. He puzzled
over how he had managed to cram so much cotton into it this
time. He couldn't figure it out, but grew increasingly proud
of his accomplishment.

"Huh!" he said to Glorianna. "Maybe you finished a
little ahead because I stopped for awhile, but just you wait
until my sack is weighed. I guess that'll prove who picked the
most."

Jaybird's father took Glorianna's sack. He weighed it. It weighed a little less than twenty pounds, about as much as her other two bags had weighed. It was about what Augustus' other bags had weighed too. But this time—Augustus swaggered up to the scales. Jaybird's father lifted the sack and a curious expression crossed his face. He put the bag on the scales and his expression grew even stranger.

"Fifty pounds!" he muttered and turned to stare at Augustus, who crowed triumphantly and shouted, "Oh boy, I guess that shows who's the best cotton picker in this family."

Mr. Hardy continued to stare at him with a peculiar seriousness and Augustus felt the beginning of a vague uneasiness. Why was he looking at him like that—and Jaybird was doing the same thing.

"Wha—what's the matter?" Augustus blurted, shuffling his feet.

"Boy," said Mr. Hardy, "I don't believe you'd cheat, but there's something mighty strange about this bag of cotton."

"Strange?" said Augustus. He was beginning to feel embarrassed. "How do you mean, strange?"

Jaybird's father shook his head. "I mean that no bag of cotton this size has any right to weigh that much." He poked at the bag. "I have known people who would put stones in a sack to make it weigh a lot so they'd get paid more," he said. "I don't think you'd do that but there's still something mighty funny here."

"Stones?" said Augustus in amazement. "Pay?" In the excitement of his competition with Glorianna he had forgotten that he was being paid for every pound of cotton he picked.

Now he realized what he was suspected of doing and his face turned bright red. He was so confused and embarrassed he could hardly talk.

"S—stones," he choked. "There's no stones in that bag." He looked helplessly at the faces around him and his own face grew even redder. "Turn it over—empty it and see." His voice was hurt and indignant.

Without a word, Mr. Hardy turned the bag upside down and began to shake out the cotton. It stuck and he reached in to pull it out. A big lump of soft white fibers tumbled out. Then another. A third mass of cotton came out of the bag and then a round hard dark object fell out and was immediately followed by a shower of other objects of about the same size and shape. They looked like stones. Augustus stared in amazement.

Mr. Hardy bent over and picked up one of the things. He held it up and looked at it. "Why," he said, "why, it's a sweet potato! There were nearly a bushel of them in there."

"Sweet—sweet potatoes?" Augustus' voice went up and down shrilly. He gaped at the potatoes that had nearly half filled his bag. "Sweet potatoes," he repeated weakly. "How did they get in there?"

Jupiter suddenly started to walk off—and then Augustus knew.

"Hey!" he yelled. "You come back here." He darted after Jupiter and grabbed him by the collar. "Look," he sputtered, "you were the only one messing around with sweet potatoes. How did you get 'em in my bag and what did you do it for?"

Jupiter wriggled, squirmed, saw that he couldn't break away and then stood quietly.

"Well," said Jupiter. "He said I could have as many 'taters as I could tote off, didn't he? Well, I just toted 'em over to your bag an' put 'em in while you were watching those ants." He shook his head sadly. "Shucks, they were kind of heavy and I thought you could carry 'em easier than I could an' then they'd get dumped in the wagon an' the wagon would go to Mr. Hardy's barn an' then the 'taters would be nearly home an' it wouldn't be so hard to tote 'em the rest of the way."

Jaybird's father looked from Jupiter to Augustus and then at the potatoes. Then he slapped his knee and bellowed with laughter.

Augustus didn't know whether to laugh or to be angry. "I'm sorry he took so many," he said. "I'll take them up to your house so you can use them."

Mr. Hardy wiped his eyes and said, "No, I know a better way to fix that young man. I'll lend you a cotton bag. We'll put all the potatoes in it and make him carry them all the way to your place. I expect they'll get sort of heavy before he gets there."

Augustus and Jaybird filled the bag. Augustus turned a stern eye on Jupiter and held the bag out to him.

Sheepishly, Jupiter slung it over his shoulder and with the potatoes bumping and thumping against the back of his legs, he started slowly down the long road home.

CHAPTER FIVE

Pop said, "I'm afraid I can't get you that pass to go through the camp. They're mighty busy down there right now. Seems there's going to be some war games around here and they won't have any time for visitors until that's all over."

"War games!" exclaimed Augustus. "Around here? Then maybe we can see 'em, huh?"

"Likely so," Pop agreed. "Seems there's goin' to be two armies, the Blues and the Reds. The Blues will be defending Camp Lee an' the Reds will be attackin' it. I've heard tell they'll be a-rampagin' around all over this section."

"Oh, boy!" Augustus' eyes shone. "Will they have tanks an' jeeps an' everythin'?"

"Will they!" Pop spread his arms wide. "Why, chop me up an' call me fish bait, never did I see such a clankin' an' a clatterin' as there is in that camp. Tanks? Jeeps? Why, they're a-racin' those things around down there a-gettin' 'em ready until a man can't breathe for the red dust, hardly."

Augustus and Jaybird were impatient. They soon decided they couldn't wait for the Army to start its maneuvers and decided to have a war game of their own. They rounded up Glorianna and Jupiter.

"You two will be the Blue Army," Augustus told them. "Jaybird and I will be the Reds ——"

"I want to be the Reds," Glorianna interrupted.

"But you can't. That's our color," Augustus explained. "We can't all be Reds."

"Don't care." Glorianna was firm. "Red is a prettier color an' I want to be it."

Augustus liked red too. That was why he had chosen it. But he knew how stubborn Glorianna could be and he wanted to get on with the war game.

"Oh, all right," he said disgustedly. "Just like a girl. What difference does the color make? Go on and be the Reds then an' we'll be the Blues."

Jupiter didn't care what his color was. He was only worried about one thing. War game or no war game he wanted to be sure to get back in time for his dinner. Augustus promised they would and Jupiter agreed to go, after thoughtfully filling his pockets with cold biscuits.

"Now you go out in the woods somewhere between here and Jaybird's house," Augustus said, "and we have to follow you and attack you."

"No fair throwin' stones," said Glorianna.

Augustus nodded.

"An' no mud balls either."

Augustus agreed to this too, but rather regretfully.

"Aw," he grumbled, "we have to have some kind of weapons an' mud balls are the nicest kind because they leave a mark an' you can prove who you hit."

Glorianna refused to appreciate the beauties of mud balls and the war was held up while Augustus searched his mind for some other weapon.

"They had a war game here before you folks came," said Jaybird. "An' the planes dropped bags of flour to show what they hit."

"Swell," said Augustus. "We can use bags of flour too." Then after a minute's thought he shook his head regretfully. "Flour costs too much," he said. "An' besides it wouldn't be right to waste food in wartime."

However, the idea stayed with him. For one thing he had a big stack of paper bags he had saved up. He went to the tent and got the bags. "Even if we can't use flour," he said, "I betcha we can fill these ol' bags with something else."

"I know," said Jaybird suddenly. "Water. That would leave a mark and it wouldn't get anyone too dirty—even a girl."

Everyone accepted this suggestion gleefully.

"The water would soak through the bags if we filled 'em now," Augustus said. "The thing to do is to take buckets of water with us an' fill the bags when we need 'em."

"Uh-huh," Jaybird said, "that way it'll be like having a supply train that we have to guard just the same as the Army."

Glorianna and Jupiter took some bags. They filled a bucket with water and lugging it between them went off to hide.

Augustus and Jaybird took a bucket apiece and went in

the opposite direction. Once in the woods they stopped to make their battle plans.

Jaybird said, "If we swing wide around them I expect we can come up on 'em from the rear and take 'em by surprise."

That agreed with the plan Augustus had been working out.

"Not only that," he said, "but we can drive 'em back toward the tent an' then we'll still be in the woods while they're out in the open." His whole face shone as he drew his arm back and threw an imaginary bag of water. "Pow!" he said. "Oh boy, just wait till I see that ol' Red Army!"

In his mind, Augustus was no longer wearing overalls. He was wearing a uniform. It bore some resemblance to that of a general in the U.S. Army, but it went beyond even that magnificence. For one thing, he had reached back into the past for big glittering gold epaulets. A huge imaginary sword dangled at his side and its hilt was covered with diamonds and rubies and emeralds. In some ways the hat he saw himself wearing was like the full-dress hat of an admiral in that it had a long ostrich plume. From there it went on to become strikingly like the pictures he had seen of pirates' hats. A big white skull and crossbones strongly suggested the fate of any enemy silly enough to encounter him.

If Augustus' imaginary uniform was somewhat gaudy, his plan of battle was a good one. He and Jaybird moved forward swiftly and silently. They knew the value of surprise and speed. The buckets of water grew heavier, but they went

on grimly, proud that they could drive their aching muscles on into greater and greater efforts. There were hills to climb and rocks to scramble over. Some of the water spilled but a good supply was left when Augustus climbed a tree and came down grinning to announce that he had seen the enemy.

"They're right where we want 'em," he said. "Right between us and the tent. Now we can crawl up and drive 'em back into the open."

No army ever went into action with greater joy. The first shot came as a complete surprise to the Red Army, which had seated itself comfortably to eat its emergency rations— the biscuits Jupiter had crammed into his pockets. The bags required some practice for accurate throwing and the first volley was more of a success as a surprise than in the effects achieved. Augustus missed Glorianna and Jaybird missed Jupiter but he did score a hit on the biscuits. This aroused Jupiter more than a hit on himself would have. He let out a shrill squeal of rage and threw bags of water in all directions. He used up so much water that Glorianna was forced to call for a retreat. She managed the retreat well, stopping sometimes for rear-guard actions that kept Augustus and Jaybird from pressing their advantage too closely.

The attacking Blues were more and more elated as they saw their strategy working out as they had hoped. Glorianna didn't see the trap and was retreating closer to the open field where the tent stood. Hits were scored on both sides and the sounds of battle rose ever louder.

The clamor reached a high point as Pop came home

from Camp Lee. Pop was tired but the noise was so unusual, even for his family, that he went out to the woods to investigate. Standing behind a tree, he watched the battle surge past him. Both armies were dripping wet by this time, partly from the enemy's fire but mostly from the water that trickled from

their own ammunition as they filled the bags and held them, watching for a target.

Pop always said that he was a man who liked to see people have fun. Moreover, he recognized fun when he saw it even if its form was a little unusual. He beamed and shouted encouragement to both armies.

"Keep a-heavin', Glorianna!" he bellowed. "That's the stuff. Why, throw me away for a fish head, you'll beat 'em yet." Then: "Keep a-comin', Augustus, keep 'em on the run. Well, I'll be a no 'count garfish if that wasn't a good shot."

Pop grew more and more excited. Besides being a man who liked to see others have fun, Pop was a man who liked to have fun himself. The strain of just watching grew too much for him and he joined the army nearest him, which happened to be the Blues. Filling a bag he heaved it and then without stopping to see the result he tore through the woods and joined up with the Reds.

Pop prided himself on being fair and ran from one army to the other, stopping just long enough to fire one shot with each. This made the battle somewhat complicated, not to say confused.

Augustus and Jaybird stuck to their plan and drove the Reds to the edge of the woods. Glorianna saw the danger too late. She tried to escape to the side to avoid being driven into the field, but the Blue Army and Pop, who happened to be on that side at the time, foiled the attempt. The Blues put on a final spirited charge and forced the Reds to break out of the woods and scurry across the field, where without cover they made wonderful targets. The Blues hastily filled their bags and threw as fast as they could, while the Reds ran to get on the other side of the tent.

Ma came out of the tent to empty a pail of dirty dishwater. Her thoughts were far away and she didn't notice Glorianna and Jupiter run past her. Neither did she notice the bag full of water that came sailing toward her. Augustus stared wide-eyed as the bag and Ma approached each other. They reached the same place at the same time and then came a loud wet "plop," as the bag burst on Ma's head and water streamed over her amazed features.

For a second Ma's amazement continued. Then she recovered herself. The Blue Army suddenly became very quiet but not before Ma had located it. Augustus and Jaybird were still in the cover of the woods, but Pop, who had led the last charge, had broken into the open. He stood there now at the edge of the field, looking rather sheepish as he held a newly filled water bag and shifted from one foot to the other.

Pop had not thrown the bag that hit Ma but unfortunately Ma had no way of knowing that.

"Well, I declare to the hills and the valleys!" Ma shouted. "So you want to play pranks, do you? All right, two can play at that game." As she spoke, Ma drew her dishwater bucket far back and then suddenly jerked it forward and let go.

The shiny tin bucket glittered in the sun as it rose after the long spout of water that flew ahead of it. The water hit Pop first. It hit him very thoroughly, running from his head

down to his feet. Then the bucket finished the job. With a tinny clank it landed on its side squarely on top of Pop's head. Then it rolled off and dribbled a little more soapy water down Pop's chin before it fell to the ground with a thump that sounded very self-satisfied.

Pop was not angry but he seemed confused for a time. He stared at Ma silently for a minute and then Augustus saw the joy of battle light his face. It was the same joy that had led Pop into the war between the Blues and Reds. Pop had enjoyed that battle and now he was ready to go on with it. His droopy, yellow mustache lifted in a wide grin. His eyes gleamed.

"Ma!" he bellowed. "I'm a rootin', tootin', bellowin' fighter from way back. Defend yourself, for I'm a-comin' at you." With that Pop let fly with the water bag he had been holding. It was a good shot. Ma looked around wildly for ammunition to return it.

Glorianna and Jupiter were quick to see that they had a chance to get powerful reinforcements. They came galloping back to Ma dragging their water bucket and bags. Glorianna filled a bag to show Ma how to do it.

The war between the Blues and Reds was about to begin again on a larger scale than before when both sides dropped their weapons and ducked as the sound of heavy gunfire broke from the woods back of them.

The fire was answered from the road. Augustus' eyes were the shape and nearly the size of small plates as he saw a long line of soldiers leave the road and scatter for cover.

The shooting started from the woods again. Augustus turned unbelievingly in that direction. Suddenly he knew what was happening.

"It's the Army war game!" he shouted. "It's started an' we're right in the middle of it!"

CHAPTER SIX

Even though Augustus knew that the volleys of shot from the woods and road were blanks, he found himself hugging the ground and looking for a hole to crawl into. For that he was angry with himself until he saw the soldiers at the roadside doing the same thing. That gave him the gratifying feeling that his actions were right and soldierly.

Machine guns were letting go now and their sharp, jarring chatter rang through the woods and fields with a sound like hundreds of enormous woodpeckers banging away at a dead limb.

The soldiers on the road wore blue arm bands so Augustus knew they were part of the army defending Camp Lee against the invading Reds. They were evidently a light scouting force sent out to find the advance units of the Reds and test their strength.

Augustus found that his sympathies were with the Blues. They were defending their camp and that was as if they were defending the United States against an invading army. The battle was going against the Blues. Augustus squirmed as he realized they had fallen into an ambush, and felt personally responsible. "How did that happen?" he asked himself.

The buzzing roar of planes overhead gave him the answer. The Red planes had discovered the Blue force on the road while the Red ground force, hidden in the woods, had not been seen by the Blue planes.

Augustus realized how well the Red soldiers had been concealed when he remembered that he had been all through those woods without seeing a sign of them. He decided that they must have been filtering in behind him as he chased Glorianna and Jupiter. In that excitement he wouldn't have noticed what was going on in his rear.

The Blues had recovered from the first surprise. They were strung out in a long thin line in the ditch beside the road and in hollows and gullies in the field.

Augustus couldn't see a soldier of either force now, but he could follow their battle lines by the rattle of gunfire from both positions.

The referees were going back and forth picking out men who would have been killed if the bullets were real. When a man was counted out he took off his steel helmet as a sign that he was out of the battle.

Augustus wriggled into a shallow gully and crawled back toward the road to be with the army he had chosen for his own. He pushed through a clump of tall grass and found himself staring at the black hole at the end of a rifle barrel.

Two men wearing blue arm bands lay in the gully.

When they saw that Augustus was not one of the Red soldiers they went on with what they had been doing. One was an officer. The other carried a big pack on his back. A metal rod jutted up from the top of it. The soldier wore earphones and was talking into a mouthpiece.

"A portable radio," Augustus thought.

The radio man said something to the officer. Augustus caught the words "tanks" and "be here in a minute."

The officer studied the woods through his binoculars, then turned quickly as a sudden burst of firing came from the side. Augustus knew what he was thinking. Somehow the Reds had crossed the field farther up and were getting ready to sweep down the road, catching the Blue forces in the side and rear.

The officer and radio man fell back toward the road. Augustus followed. The radio man talked into his mouthpiece as he went. Augustus heard the officer say, "If the tanks get here in time we'll crack them wide open."

A low growl and a clanking sound drew Augustus' attention. The sounds grew louder, became a steady roar. Big lumbering shapes appeared down the road and swept across the field. Small trees in the path of the hurtling forms cracked and disappeared.

Augustus jumped up and waved his arms. "Yay!" he yelled. "The tanks—now we'll show 'em."

The Blue line was not moving back now. It was charging ahead. Augustus saw a group of Reds dodge through the woods, trying to avoid a tank. Augustus grinned triumphantly. Then his grin faded. The tank was no longer crashing ahead, mowing down everything in its way. The roaring of the motor had become a coughing sputter. The tank was barely moving now. The motor gasped, puffed a few times and stopped.

The Reds swarmed back, throwing hand grenades. They rushed up a small cannon. A referee dashed in and said the tank was out of action.

"Just wait!" Augustus yelled. "Our other tanks'll be here in a minute and then you'll see!"

The other tanks were coming. Or were they? Augustus scowled in dismay as he saw that one had stopped halfway across the field. Another one charged up, reached the edge of the woods and then it began to cough and sputter. It stopped. For a moment Reds and Blues were mixed in a wild confusion and then the referees were waving their arms, shouting to stop the action.

One tank still rolled toward the woods, but dotted across the field and on the road, the other great grim shapes were still as dead monsters. Augustus ran toward one of the tanks. Jaybird was beside him when he got there.

Augustus had lost track of Jaybird in the excitement. Turning to him now, he gasped, "What happened?"

Jaybird shook his head. "Dunno."

Soldiers crawled out of the tanks and poked into the depths of the great heavy machinery. Augustus heard a group of officers talking. "Our mechanized units are stalled all along the road—tanks, trucks, scout cars, everything.

"It's sabotage all right—too many of them to be an accident."

"Sabotage!" That meant someone had been able to disable the Army's equipment deliberately. Augustus felt a sense of shock greater than anything he had ever known. Why, if the enemy could get into an Army camp and do this, nothing was safe. And if they could do it here while the Army was on maneuvers maybe they could wreck the tanks and trucks that were going into actual battle.

A soldier who had been working on a tank motor came up to the officers. He rubbed his thumb and forefinger together, sniffed at them and nodded.

"It's wax," he said. "Someone has put wax in our gasoline."

Wax in the gasoline! Augustus stared. Wax? What would that do?

"Wax dissolves in gas," the soldier went on. "When it gets down into the motor it sticks to the metal, makes a coating on the cylinder walls, blocks up the carburetor ——" His eyes glinted. "I'd like to know who did it."

Augustus grabbed Jaybird's arm. "You hear that?" he asked.

Jaybird nodded.

"Well, we want to help the Army, don't we?" Augustus demanded.

Jaybird nodded again.

"Then here's our chance." Augustus' voice cracked. "We've got to find out who put that wax in the gas."

Jaybird looked doubtful. "Yeh," he said. "But how we going to do that?"

Augustus didn't answer his question. Instead he said,

"We'll show 'em. Just wait. Just wait till I find those ol' spies."

Augustus and Jaybird watched the men take the motors apart and clean them. Everywhere it was the same story—wax.

It all seemed like a bad dream to Augustus. A dream that lasted all day and far into the night when glaring lights dotted the woods and fields and the clank and clatter of men working with metal rang over the usually quiet hillside.

In the morning everything had gone. If it hadn't been for the deep ruts and broken bushes, Augustus would not have been sure that it had all happened.

When Pop came home from working at the camp, he said, "Never in all my born days did I see such a mad lot of men and guards—why, fry me for a catfish, you can't as much as look at those gas tanks without six of 'em pop out an' get ready to grab you!"

Augustus nudged Jaybird. "I betcha they don't put the wax in the gas tanks at all," he said.

Jaybird looked hard at nothing.

"Then how do they get it in?" he asked.

Augustus scratched his head. "Maybe they've got some kind of an ol' secret weapon," he said mysteriously. "You know, the Germans are always saying they've got 'em an' maybe they're usin' one now."

Jaybird's expression brightened. "I've got a book about weapons," he said. "All kinds. I don't know if any of 'em are secret but it's a big book with pictures and it belonged to my grandfather."

Augustus looked interested. "Let's get it," he said.

On the way to Jaybird's house Augustus stopped.

"Look," he said. "If we're goin' to catch someone who's using secret weapons we have to be secret ourselves an' not go walkin' along a road where everyone can see us."

Jaybird said, "But we're just going to my house."

"Yeh, I know." Augustus' voice suggested untold mysteries. "But we'd better start bein' secret about everything." He looked around carefully. "Tell you what," he said. "We'll make a secret trail through the woods to your house."

When the trail was laid out, it was a path through the thickest woods Augustus could find. At one point it led through a clump of Spanish bayonet. The stiff spear-shaped leaves of this bristly growth, ending in points sharp as needles, seemed to Augustus to be the perfect cover for a secret trail.

In fact, after he had stabbed himself twice on the hard points, he decided this was the place to have a secret meeting place.

"It'll be swell," he said. "No one can sneak up on us through those ol' bayonets while we're making plans and things."

They hacked an opening in the middle of the bristling growth and built a small hut of branches.

"There," said Augustus when it was finished. "Now we have a secret trail and a secret meeting place for our headquarters." He nodded proudly. "Now we're really getting started right."

Augustus waited in the headquarters while Jaybird

went home and came back with his book about weapons.

They studied it carefully but although it had descriptions and pictures of about every known weapon from ancient times up to the period of the Civil War, it was strangely lacking in any mention of secret weapons.

"I guess it's just not modern enough," said Augustus. "After all, it doesn't say anything about tanks or planes either so I guess secret weapons prob'ly weren't invented when this book was printed."

In spite of that it was an interesting old book and they examined it until dark. Augustus had never before seen pictures of the weapons of ancient times, before gunpowder was invented. He knew about bows and arrows, swords and spears, but the big siege weapons that took the place of artillery in those old days were new to him.

"Maybe we could use some of these things some time," he said. "Boy, wouldn't that be a swell thing for smashing doors in." He pointed to a picture of a battering ram—a huge log hung on ropes from a sturdy frame.

"Yeh," said Jaybird. "That's what they used for breaking down walls and castle gates."

"An' look at this one." Augustus pointed to a catapult used for slinging great rocks. "We could make one of those just by bending a small tree an' then letting it snap up again —Boy, I'm sorry we didn't think of that when we had the battle with Glorianna an' Jupiter."

When darkness filtered through the woods, Augustus realized that they had not made much progress toward a plan to uncover the spies who had disabled the tanks and trucks.

"Well," he said hopefully, "we've got a good secret headquarters anyway. I'll meet you here in the morning and we'll think up a plan sure as anything."

"All right." Jaybird was going down the trail when Augustus' call stopped him.

"Remember," said Augustus, "don't let anyone see you coming here. An' if you meet up with any spies on the way, why, just lead 'em off in some other direction."

"Uh-huh," said Jaybird. He spent the rest of his walk home wondering how he would know a spy if he saw one, and in which other direction to lead him. He also wondered what the spy might do while he was being led.

CHAPTER SEVEN

Jaybird thought Augustus had a gun in his hand as he crawled through the bushes that masked the entrance to their secret trail. Whatever it was that Augustus was carrying, the early morning sunlight glinted from it with a glitter as bright as that from any gun barrel. Jaybird hurried to the edge of the woods to investigate.

Augustus' gait was a cross between a hop and a gallop and his whole attitude indicated that his mind was crowded with matters of more than ordinary importance.

"Look," he said, thrusting his hand out toward Jaybird. "I forgot I had these good ol' binoculars. Cap'n Parker gave 'em to me up in Maine."

Jaybird saw that the light glittering on the glasses of the binoculars was what had made him think Augustus was carrying a gun.

"What you fixin' to do with 'em?" he asked, taking the binoculars and peering through them.

"Do with 'em? Why, don't you see—all we have to do is to go up on a hill an' with these ol' spyglasses we can see the whole camp. If we watch long enough we can see who's monkeyin' with the gasoline."

"Thunder Hill's nearest to the camp an' it's a far piece from there—nearly a mile away," Jaybird said. "Can we see that far with these ——?" He stopped and bending over picked up a stone and threw it.

Augustus didn't see anything worth throwing a stone at.

Jaybird looked sheepish. "I forgot I was lookin' through those things," he said. "I saw a buzzard on that dead tree way over yonder an' he looked so close I thought I could hit him easy as anything."

The tree was so far off that without the glasses the buzzard was a tiny black dot.

"Well, I guess that shows you," Augustus said. "We can see the camp from Thunder Hill easy."

"Yeh." Jaybird sounded convinced and hopeful. "An' we can see the whole camp, not just one little part of it like the guards do. We'll see what's goin' on back of the guards an' all around everywhere."

They narrowed their eyes at each other and wriggled excitedly.

Augustus said, "We'd better get started. You can't tell, someone might be putting wax in the gasoline right now."

"Just let me catch 'em, that's all," Jaybird said, scowling fiercely and punching violently at the air to prove that any German spy, no matter how big, could expect no mercy from him.

When they started for Thunder Hill, Jaybird was wise enough to stop at his house to pick up some lunch. He knew

Augustus would want to stay all day and he knew too that Augustus hadn't thought of lunch and wouldn't want to go back to get any.

They could have reached the hill overlooking the camp in not more than an hour by taking the road in the valley. Neither of them suggested that. Without a word they set off to follow the densely wooded ridge that curved in a wide semicircle, adding miles to the distance to be covered. The disadvantages of this route were more than made up for by the greater satisfaction of skulking mysteriously through the woods, stopping now and then to climb a tree and peer around with the binoculars to make sure the enemy was not trailing them.

"You can't ever tell where they might be," Augustus whispered. "They're smart so we have to be smarter."

Coming to a shallow stream that flowed in the right direction, Augustus rolled up his overalls and walked in the water.

"This'll throw 'em off the track if they're followin' us," he said.

Jaybird nodded admiringly, wishing he had thought up such a good idea. When the stream turned away from their course, the way led through a thick brier patch. The enemy was temporarily forgotten as Jaybird picked his way carefully through the briers, feeling cautiously with his bare feet before putting his weight down.

Augustus scornfully announced that that was no way to go through a brier patch. "This is the way I do," he said, and closing his eyes, he ran through the briers as fast as he could.

The progress of both Augustus and Jaybird was punctuated by a practically continuous stream of "ouches," but once past the briers each was still insisting that his own method was better.

"I miss most of 'em," said Jaybird. "An' you step on 'em all."

"Shucks," said Augustus, "it takes me only half as long so it only hurts half as much."

Both pairs of legs seemed to be equally scratched and the difference of opinion was still unsettled when Jaybird said, "Shhh! That's Thunder Hill right ahead."

Thunder Hill was just a high point of the ridge they had been following. On one side, it sloped steeply toward the camp in the valley below. On the other, the slope was gradual and dotted with isolated farms reached by narrow country roads.

Augustus and Jaybird crept through the woods, stopping every now and then to raise a hand warningly and say, "Shhh," at each other. Accustomed to the half-darkness under the trees, Augustus was startled when he pushed through a mass of thick underbrush and came out in the bright light of a cleared space. It was a very unusual clearing. Not wider than a road, it was like a road in length. Starting near the camp in the valley the long narrow clearing ran straight up the side of Thunder Hill, over the top and down the gradual slope of the other side. Apart from a narrow mound of red dirt running through the middle of the long

clearing, the ground was undisturbed and rough, with no sign of the leveling or smoothing that would have been done for a road.

Augustus hesitated and looked up and down. There was no one in sight in the clearing. The camp lay at the foot of it and, with no trees or bushes between, the view was perfect. This was an unexpected piece of luck. Augustus started to ask Jaybird what the clearing was for, but something else crowded the question from his mind. Augustus had expected he would have to climb a tree to see the camp. And right in front of him, on the other side of the clearing, was just the kind of tree he had hoped to find. It was a tall pine rising high above all the surrounding trees. It would be satisfyingly hard but not impossible to climb up to where the branches clustered thickly. From there it would be easy to get up to where a high crotch provided the right foundation for something Augustus had been looking forward to building—a tree hut.

In his mind he had seen himself and Jaybird snugly perched in a leafy shelter high above the ground and safe from the counterspying of any lurking enemy who happened to be walking over Thunder Hill. It was a pleasant picture and Augustus rebelled at the idea of giving it up. Besides, he had brought along a rope for the express purpose of lifting up branches for the hut's construction. He convinced himself, and tried to convince Jaybird, that just to sit on the ground in the long clearing would be unworthy of any scout, from Dan'l Boone on down.

"Why, looka there," Augustus said. "Just see for yourself. Why, any ol' enemy that came along could see us sittin' here in this clearing looking at them with our spyglass. An' when they saw us sittin' here watching 'em do you suppose they'd be foolish enough to do anythin' wrong so we could catch 'em at it?" He snorted derisively. "Not those ol' spies; they're too smart."

Jaybird seemed partly convinced and Augustus went on triumphantly, "Why, we could cama— cam— camouflage a tree hut so no one would ever see it."

The word "camouflage" had a profound effect on Augustus and Jaybird. They had both seen examples of this art in newspaper photographs. The word itself had a satisfyingly important sound and hinted at mysteries only half understood. It probably carried the day against Jaybird's lack of enthusiasm for lugging heavy objects up into the treetops, because he was soon co-operating eagerly in the work of finding strong poles for the floor of the hut.

CHAPTER EIGHT

They both had knives, rather dull ones, and with these as their only tools, it took quite a lot of time and effort to hack down branches that were strong enough to make a secure platform. Their hands were red and blistered and there was a place between the thumb and forefinger of Augustus' right hand where the skin was worn away altogether. Augustus looked at this place with pride. It was like being wounded, he felt, and he squeezed his thumb against its soreness just to prove to himself that he didn't mind a little pain.

The next step was to hoist the cut branches up into the tree and Augustus volunteered to do that. He climbed up to the crotch he had picked for the hut's support. Sitting on one of the limbs, he lowered his rope's end to the ground. Jaybird tied the rope around a bundle of branches and Augustus pulled them up, tugging hard to get them past limbs that seemed to take a spiteful joy in catching on the bundle.

The place Augustus had chosen was a good one. The branches that spread out from the crotch provided a solid, level base and Augustus soon had the floor poles lashed in place. He found he had used up a lot of his rope to lash them and had to go halfway down the tree to get the shortened

rope down to Jaybird. He didn't mind the extra trouble because the really interesting part of making the tree hut was
coming.

"Now for the cam— camouflage," he said.

Jaybird tied some branches to the rope but Augustus
stopped him.

"Hey," he said, "what kind of a crazy ol' camouflage
would that be? You've got some oak boughs in there an' who
ever heard of oak leaves in a pine tree?"

Jaybird looked around as if trying to find someone else
to blame for this oversight. Not finding anyone, he went off
to cut some more pine boughs.

When the hut was finished, Augustus slid down the
tree and he and Jaybird stood looking up at it.

"Why, I can't tell it from the rest of the tree," Jaybird
said.

Augustus smiled proudly, feeling repaid for all his
work. "An' you know it's there," he said. "What chance
would any ol' spy have of seeing it?"

Satisfied that their work was good, Augustus and Jaybird climbed up to their hut and sat under the fragrant shelter
of its woven pine branches. Augustus had left some window
openings and they took turns watching the camp with the
binoculars.

From their height they could see every part of the big
camp. A strong breeze rocked the treetop, rustling the pine
needles and giving the tree hut the swing and sway of a small
boat on long rolling waves. When Augustus had the binoculars, it was easy enough for him to keep his mind on the duty

of watching the camp. When it was Jaybird's turn with the glasses, Augustus sometimes found his attention wandering pleasantly to other subjects—the pungent smell of the pine needles, a big yellow butterfly that was caught in an upward current of air and fluttered through a window opening to light on Augustus' knee. The butterfly's wings were marked with a strange black design and Augustus wondered if spies ever used butterflies to carry messages in the way carrier pigeons are used. He tried to find some hidden meaning in the markings on the butterfly's wings but was interrupted in that task when the butterfly flew away and swooped gracefully down to the ground. For some reason that reminded Augustus of the time he had trained a frog to do parachute jumping. And with parachutes on his mind, Augustus pretended he was going down with one and studied the ground for a good place to land. He decided the long roadlike clearing was the only place and then started to wonder about the clearing. He remembered that he had been on the point of asking Jaybird what it was for and had then forgotten about it in the excitement of building the tree hut.

"Hey, Jaybird," he said, "what's that long clearing for anyway?"

Jaybird turned from watching the camp, proud of his knowledge of the mysterious cleared place. "That's the pipe line," he said.

"Pipe line?" Augustus' tone was puzzled. "What's a pipe line?"

Jaybird was happy to air his knowledge. "Oh, it's a big ol' pipe that runs underground all the way from Louisiana.

They pump oil and gasoline through it way up here an' even farther—way up north."

"Oil?" Augustus asked. "Gasoline?"

"Yeh, you see that long mound of dirt? Well, the pipe is down under that. I saw them dig the ditch for it an' put the pipe down, last year, before you came." He pointed toward the back side of the hill. "The main line from Louisiana to the North goes up that way. This one here is just a little branch line they hooked on an' it just goes from the main line to the camp." He shook his head earnestly. "Boy, it sure was a big job diggin' her an' layin' that pipe. I was up here nearly every day watching an' I talked to all the men an' they told me all about it an' how it works."

Augustus looked at the long mound of red dirt, and pulled his left ear thoughtfully. Jaybird turned back to resume his watch of the camp. Augustus sat silently. He stopped pulling his left ear and started on the right one.

"Yeh," he said after a while. "It must have been a big job. How deep did they have to dig the ditch for all that pipe?"

Jaybird answered casually, "Oh, about three feet, I guess. Say, you should have seen the big ol' thing that dug that ditch. Sort of like a tractor it was, only maybe more like a plow. Anyway, that thing sure tore up the ground."

Augustus said, "Hm." Then he added, "Gasoline for the camp." He inspected the long cleared lane carefully.

When it was Augustus' time to watch the camp, he turned the binoculars on the big gasoline tanks and the soldiers guarding them. Everything seemed to be all right there and he focused the glasses to other parts of the camp. He watched all the buildings and the men who entered and left them.

He switched to the unfinished buildings to watch the men at work building them.

"Maybe I'll see Pop," he thought. He didn't see Pop. He didn't see any workmen at all. He was wondering about that when he realized that the light was getting dim. "Huh," he said in surprise. "It's getting late; guess they've all gone home."

Augustus lingered over every detail of the camp and then to Jaybird's astonishment he turned his glasses on the cleared pipe-line lane and followed it from the camp up the hill and back over the crest to the slope beyond.

"Hey!" Jaybird said. "What you doing?"

Augustus waved a hand for silence and carefully inspected the woods on both sides of the pipe-line clearing.

Jaybird suddenly realized that the sun had set and he remembered that it was a long way home even if they followed the short road through the valley.

"Look," he said, "maybe we better stop for today and come back tomorrow."

Again Augustus waved a hand for silence. The light had faded quickly after the sun vanished beyond the hills and Augustus' binoculars were trained intently on a spot in the woods just outside the cleared lane. He focused the glasses again and again as darkness crept up swiftly.

"There's someone hiding there in the woods," he whispered. "More than one of them—an' what I want to know is what are they doing hiding out in the woods just when it's getting dark."

Jaybird felt a prickling sensation run over him. He remembered Augustus' interest in the pipe line, the pipe line that brought the gasoline to the camp. He leaned forward excitedly, trying to see through the binoculars with Augustus. He knew now why Augustus had turned the glasses in that direction. No one had been able to find anything wrong at the gasoline tanks, but here was the pipe that fed the tanks.

"What are they doing?" Jaybird whispered.

Augustus didn't answer.

It grew darker and darker.

Augustus murmured, "Here they come. They're sneaking out of the woods. Now they're in the clearing." His voice grew tense. "Now they're stopping at the ditch where the pipe is buried——" His voice trailed off and he turned to Jaybird, his eyes popping. "Jaybird," he whispered, "they've got some bags with them and they're digging right where the pipe runs."

Jaybird's mouth hung open and he was breathing rapidly.

"Whu—whu—" he stammered. "Whu—why?"

Augustus' eyes glittered in the darkness. "Why do you suppose?" he asked significantly.

CHAPTER NINE

It was too dark to see anything in the pipe-line clearing, even with the help of the binoculars. Augustus' straining ears caught the muffled thud of a shovel and occasionally a small clink as it hit a stone.

"What can we do?" Jaybird's whisper was shaky.

Augustus didn't know what they could do, so he didn't answer. That was the only reason his voice wasn't as shaky as Jaybird's.

After a long silence Jaybird suggested, "If we could get down to the camp an' tell the soldiers, they'd fix 'em."

Augustus wanted to take Jaybird's suggestion. He wanted to slip quietly down the tree and run to the camp. He definitely did not want to get any nearer the men in the clearing. So he was surprised to hear himself say, "Take too long—they'd be gone by the time the soldiers got here. Come on, we've got to sneak up on 'em and stop 'em our-selves."

"Stop 'em?" Jaybird gasped. "How?"

"You'll see." Augustus intended this to be reassuring but it didn't sound that way because he didn't have the slightest idea what it was that Jaybird would see. But now that he had started something Augustus had to go ahead. He crossed the hut to the tree trunk and started to climb quietly down.

Jaybird whispered, "Hey!" but Augustus didn't hesitate. There was nothing for Jaybird to do but follow. When he started, he found, as Augustus had, that getting started was the worst.

When they reached the ground both Augustus and Jaybird discovered that they were more excited than scared. The thrill of action lifted their spirits and silently they slipped through the bushes toward the sound of the shovel biting into earth.

The stars had popped out but the moon had not yet risen and under the trees everything was blank, black darkness. Augustus led the way slowly, feeling with his hands for branches ahead and letting his weight down slowly until he was sure there was nothing under his feet that would make a noise. He used a trick he had learned in the Maine woods, watching the sky for clear places between trees and following them as if they made up a path on the ground. That kept him from bumping into tree trunks but the only way to avoid bushes was to feel his way around them. He was afraid he would get separated from Jaybird and whispered to him to hold onto the back of his overalls.

Step by step he crept closer to the sounds until finally he could make out some dim shapes in the clearing. The gray darkness in the clearing was enough lighter than the black darkness under the trees so that Augustus could finally identify the shapes he saw as men.

He stopped at the edge of the woods and watched. He could make out the movements of the man with the shovel. Then the shoveling stopped and the man said, "Got it, Joe." The words were good slangy American but the voice was high-pitched with a harsh, grating quality that was different from anything Augustus had heard before. He would not have been surprised by a German accent but this unknown one puzzled him.

"Good, get the cover off, Tojo. Hermann, you help me with the bags." This voice was more like what Augustus had been expecting. It could have been American except for just a trace of Germanic heaviness.

But what the voice said brought Augustus upright with a jerk. "Tojo"—that meant the first voice belonged to a Jap. Augustus felt Jaybird's shoulder press against him and knew Jaybird had heard too. Joe and Hermann would be Germans. Two Germans and a Jap!

Augustus remembered the stories he had heard of Japanese cruelty and felt a chill. The chill turned to hot anger when the Jap giggled. "He-he, Americans are so stupid."

Augustus found himself reaching for a rock to throw toward the sneering voice but caught himself in time. That would do no good, and maybe this Jap would—— Augustus forced himself to stop thinking about Japanese cruelties. He reminded himself fiercely that the thing for him to do now was to think up some way to stop these men.

"I'll show you who's stupid," he thought but although he wrinkled his forehead and pulled both ears he couldn't think how he was going to show them.

He heard a metallic grating and the Jap said, "Cover's off."

Augustus saw him lift something and lay it on the ground. It was clear now that the men would not have to drill a hole in the pipe line. The hole had already been drilled and fitted with a cover.

A thin wedge of moon was rising now. By its faint light Augustus could make out the forms in the clearing a little more clearly. He still couldn't make out exactly what they were doing and decided to take a chance on crawling closer. He would have to be closer anyway, to do something to stop them. He wriggled through a black screen of small cedars and Spanish bayonet. The sharp leaves of the Spanish bayonet scratched his face. He looked up to locate a cleared space and saw over his head a round shape, like a big toy balloon. It was attached to a branch and swayed gently in the slight breeze. Augustus knew what it was and ducked although the thing would have been a little too high to touch even if he had been standing upright.

He felt Jaybird's hand squeeze his arm and heard him whisper, "Hornets' nest."

Augustus grinned at the alarm in Jaybird's whisper and at his own action in ducking. Here they were, he thought, crawling closer and closer to a terrible danger—and being scared by a hornets' nest! Augustus was sure that hornet

stings would be nothing compared to what the Jap would do if they were caught. Suddenly aware of complete silence in the clearing, Augustus looked that way and immediately tried to press himself down into the earth.

A short squatty figure that could only be the Jap was walking down the clearing, stopping sometimes to step into the edge of the woods and peer closely into the shadows.

One of the Germans called softly, "Oh, come back, Tojo, there is no one there."

The Jap continued his search. "Oh yeah? Well, I'll just have a look anyway."

His voice was shockingly close now. Augustus and Jaybird had crawled past the screen of small cedars and were lying in an open space beyond. Augustus knew they would be seen. There was only one thing to do. His mouth was dry as he pushed hard against Jaybird's shoulder, hoping he would understand. The Jap was too close to chance even a whisper. Jaybird understood and wormed his way backward. Together they slid back into the black shadows of the cedars and Spanish bayonet. Augustus didn't even feel the sharp leaves pricking his feet and legs.

The Jap was walking down the clearing nearly opposite him now. With the black trees around them, Augustus and Jaybird lay breathlessly waiting. The Jap stopped. Augustus knew that the very darkness of his hiding place would make it suspicious. He was suddenly sure that the Jap would look into those dark shadows. He didn't have long to wait. The squatty figure left the clearing and pushed into the edge of the woods. Already he was close enough to see Augustus and Jaybird when his eyes grew accustomed to the darkness. If he came any closer . . . Augustus tensed every muscle, ready to jump and run if the Jap took another step.

The man twisted his shoulders sideways to squeeze through the thick cedars. He thrust a hand forward to part the branches. For a moment Augustus saw his face clearly as it slowly followed the hand. Even in that dim light the heavy features looked coldly brutal. The thick lips, drawn into a snarling grin, seemed to fill all the space below the broad bulging cheekbones. Small glittering eyes probed the branches of Augustus' hiding place. Now the eyes were staring straight at Augustus. Augustus drew his foot back to kick Jaybird into a fast break to get away.

CHAPTER TEN

The Jap's hand pushed farther forward, then stopped with a jerk as a sharp cry rose above the pounding of Augustus' heart. For a moment Augustus thought maybe he had made the noise but it continued and he knew it came from the Jap. The man twisted sideways, yelped again and jumped backward. Another squawl like a startled cat's sounded briefly and then with a floundering in the underbrush the man had pushed back out of the woods and was standing in the clearing, grunting angrily. He spat out a few words that sounded like static on a radio and then spoke English again.

"Spanish bayonet," he hissed. "The second time to-night I've run into that stuff. No one but a fool would go through these woods at night."

He swung his arms viciously and stamped back to where the two Germans were waiting. Augustus saw a thick bristling clump of Spanish bayonet just ahead of him and reached forward to pat it fondly—but very gently.

One of the Germans said, "Well, Tojo, satisfied?"

The Jap snarled at him and grated, "Where's the wax? Let's get started."

Augustus and Jaybird rose to their knees and tried to follow the men's movements but had to crawl to the edge of the clearing before they could make out what was going on. They moved slowly and with a friendly respect for the clumps of Spanish bayonet. Crouching behind the last small cedar on the edge of the pipe-line clearing, Augustus divided his attention between watching the men and trying to think of a way to stop them.

His thoughts churned like water rushing through a rapids but with no more result than that produced by the water swirling on the rocks. He tried to figure out a way to use the Spanish bayonets that had already served so well and for a while seriously considered a wild scheme of tying a clump of the sharp bladelike leaves to a long pole and jabbing the men with it. He soon saw the flaws in that and groped for something else.

The men were grouped closely together and were silent except for an occasional mumble, so low that no words could be distinguished.

Augustus' mind still refused to produce an idea, and he was close to despair when he suddenly remembered that in a similar condition generals call a conference of all their officers with the hope that out of the meeting of many minds the needed idea may emerge. It was clearly impossible to talk things over with Jaybird so close to the enemy, and Augustus risked a whisper to ask him to fall back to a less exposed position.

They crawled back to the hiding place in the cedars.

This was close enough to the enemy so they could tell if anything unusual was developing, but far enough away to allow some whispered conversation.

Jaybird said, "We'd better do something right away."

"Yeh," said Augustus thoughtfully, "that's a good idea."

"Come on then, let's do it."

Augustus squinted at him and said, "Do what?"

Jaybird's whisper was impatient. "Well, do what you said—you said you'd show me."

"Oh, that?" Augustus felt hopelessly trapped now. He remembered the boast he had made, relying on getting an idea that hadn't come.

Jaybird sensed his confusion and said, "Well, I thought you had a secret weapon or something."

"Oh, sure, sure," Augustus said meaninglessly, as he stared up at the sky, hoping to see an idea float overhead. There was something over his head. It wasn't floating exactly but it did look like a balloon. Augustus had seen it before, when he and Jaybird first crawled into this place. He stared at it and pulled his left ear. Then he pulled the right one.

"Secret weapon," he murmured and a new note had crept into his voice. Jaybird started to say something but Augustus grabbed him saying, *"Shh."*

Jaybird looked around in a startled manner, thinking that Augustus had seen someone coming. But Augustus was just concentrating fiercely, trying to shut every interruption out of his mind as he followed up a thought that had burst on

him like the flood of light from a photographer's flash bulb. He pounded his knee with one hand and gripped Jaybird tighter with the fingers of the other.

"Look," he said, too loudly for safety, "look—there's our secret weapon." He pointed up at the round object overhead.

Jaybird looked. "The hornets' nest," he said slowly, remembering that he had seen it before. "But how———?"

Augustus said, "Stay here. I'll be right back," and crawled away toward the clearing.

Near the edge of the woods he stopped and it seemed to Jaybird that he was inspecting the trees.

When Augustus crawled back his whisper was joyous. "Found one that's just right."

Jaybird stared. "Right for what?"

"A cata———" Augustus gulped, groping for the word he wanted. "You know," he went on, "one of those things in your book—the things that throw things. Cat—cata— catapult." He got it out at last triumphantly.

"Oh, those." For a second Jaybird was puzzled, but then he knew, even before Augustus explained.

"Yeh," Augustus said breathlessly. "One of those. There's a good springy little tree up there that's just right. We bend it way over, hold the ol' hornet's nest against it, let go—an' *pow* it hits those spies an' there's mad hornets all over 'em."

Jaybird was still gasping with admiration as Augustus started carefully up the tree that held the hornets' nest. It was

on a low limb that Augustus soon reached and sat on as he opened his knife.

Now that he was so near the hornets' nest he remembered that the hornets might not be any more friendly toward him than they would be toward the enemy. He hesitated, but the thought of the greater danger from the Jap and the Germans drove him on. Even so, his hand was trembling a little as he reached out to cut the twig that held the nest. He cut it slowly so there would be no jerk, and as far away from the nest as possible. When his knife had made a deep V-shaped groove, he gently bent the twig until it snapped. Slowly and cautiously he slid to the ground holding the nest at arm's length and watching it intently.

"Come on," he said to Jaybird. "We better hurry or these will wake up." Getting the hornets' nest to the edge of the clearing was a ticklish job. "If it gets hit by a branch——" said Augustus warningly.

Jaybird understood and went first to hold back the branches. They crept to the tree Augustus had picked for the catapult. It was on the edge of the clearing and Augustus knew it could be seen by the enemy. He and Jaybird watched the dark shapes of the men still clustered together at the hole in the pipe line. It was impossible to tell which way the men were facing.

Augustus waited a minute and then whispered, "We'll have to take a chance." Slowly he and Jaybird stood erect. They grasped the tree as high up as they could reach and put all their weight into a slow steady pull. The tree resisted and it seemed that it might be too stiff to bend. Augustus dug his heels into the ground and pulled harder. Slowly the tree bent. Back and back it came, springing and quivering until Augustus was sure it would snap out of his hands before he was ready.

"Hold hard," he gasped and holding on with his elbows, he placed the hornets' nest against the side nearest the men. He held it there for a second as he and Jaybird gave one more tug to get even more snap when the tree flew back.

"Let go," Augustus grunted and he and Jaybird dropped to the ground as the tree whipped up with a thrumming sound.

Augustus held his breath as the round gray shape of the hornets' nest snapped out into the air and swished across the clearing.

CHAPTER ELEVEN

For a moment the hornets' nest was silhouetted against the sky and then as it curved downward it was lost against the dark mass of the trees. The calm quiet of the woods was unbroken. . . . Then, "What's that?" Another brief silence. "Uh! I'm shot!" Another voice broke in wildly: "Ow, they got me!" Sharp yelps of pain broke out in three voices and with the wild outcry came thuds and crashing noises in the underbrush. The noise grew louder, more confused. The thrashing in the bushes grew frenzied. The combined sounds reached a new high pitch and then began to fade away in the distance.

Augustus and Jaybird were on their feet staring intently where the sounds grew fainter and fainter. The last loud noise Augustus heard was a shrill "Ouch" in a voice unmistakably Japanese.

"Yay!" shouted Augustus. "I guess we fixed 'em. I guess we showed 'em an' ol' secret weapon." He pounded Jaybird happily on the back, stopped suddenly to slap wildly at the seat of his overalls and yell "Ouch," nearly as loudly as the Jap.

Jaybird didn't need to be told what to do. He turned and ran and Augustus was right at his heels. Feeling no more hornet stings, they stopped after a while, panting heavily.

"Well," Jaybird puffed, "now we can go down to the camp an' tell them about everything an' they'll come up here an' catch those fellows, I betcha."

Augustus rubbed his hornet sting thoughtfully and looked down the hill where the lights of the camp glimmered. Then he looked back where the howls and crashes of the enemy's retreat had died away on the back side of the ridge.

Jaybird recognized the stubbornness in Augustus' voice when he heard, "Naw, they'd get away. We've got to catch 'em."

"Huh? Us?" Jaybird flung his arms wide as if he were calling on all the night to hear the unreasonableness of Augustus' idea. "How?" he blurted. "How, I'm askin' you?"

Augustus shook his head. "Yeh, I know, but look." He poked a finger straight out and jabbed it at Jaybird's chest. Or rather he intended to jab Jaybird's chest just for emphasis, but in the darkness he miscalculated and stuck the finger into the pit of Jaybird's stomach. Jaybird doubled up and said, "Upf." Augustus paid no attention to this little accident and jabbed again, this time with better luck as Jaybird's chest was lower as a result of his doubling up.

"Look," Augustus repeated, "if we go way down to the camp those men will get away an' maybe no one will ever catch them an' they can just go on doin' things like spoilin'

the gas, only maybe next time they'll do somethin' even worse."

Jaybird got his breath back and sputtered, "Yeh, but how can we catch 'em? Maybe they'll catch us. And anyway how can they do anythin' worse than spoilin' the gas?"

Augustus scowled. "Prob'ly they'll burn your house down," he said.

Jaybird was so impressed by Augustus' tone of gloomy certainty that he turned to look for flames up the valley. This was not lost on Augustus and he pressed his advantage.

"An' prob'ly they'll scalp your whole family," he went on. "An' prob'ly they'll make 'em walk the plank until they're drowned."

The fact that his terrible prophecies were a little mixed up, being concerned more with Indians and pirates than Japanese and Germans, did not occur to either Augustus or Jaybird. And neither did they consider that the nearest ocean for plank-walking purposes was several hundred miles away. The threats themselves were evil enough to make Jaybird shudder for his family's safety and that was what Augustus wanted.

"Well," he demanded, "you want to see that happen?"

Jaybird said, "No," very positively.

"All right," said Augustus. "Come on then an' we'll stop it."

Jaybird was still doubtful about how all those awful things could happen and how he and Augustus could prevent them, but there didn't seem to be anything else to do but follow along when Augustus started off through the woods.

"Better circle around where those hornets are," Augustus muttered and they made a wide detour.

"Where you fixin' to go anyway?" Jaybird asked.

"Goin' to follow those spies," Augustus said determinedly.

They swung far out to avoid the hornet-infested area and then cut back to follow the pipe-line clearing as it ran over the top of the hill and dipped down the other side. They kept off the clearing itself, walking in the woods to the side so they would not be seen if the enemy came back.

Augustus wasn't even thinking of what he would do if they caught up with the men. He was devoting all his attention to finding them and that was enough of a problem for any one time. He knew they had run back over the hilltop in the direction he was following. What they had done then was another matter. They had thought the hornet stings were bullet wounds at first but how long had it taken them to learn the truth and what would they do then? Did they have a hideaway somewhere in the woods near by and if so had they gone there? And if they had, where was it? Augustus swung along, considering these questions and dozens more.

It was a fine night for scouting, clear and so still that Augustus could hear a rooster crow on some far-off unseen farm. He wondered if the people on the farm had heard all the commotion on the hill. Then he wondered if the farm might be the spies' hideout. He turned in the direction the rooster's crow had come from. There would be watchdogs at the farm, he guessed. If it really was the spies' hideout they would probably be big and unpleasant watchdogs. He considered how to avoid the dogs and creep up on the farmhouse. The rooster crowed again and Augustus knew the farm must be a long way off. It was a little more to the left than the direction in which he was going. He turned that way, still thinking about watchdogs.

The bank he found himself plunging down was a steep wall of clay. There had been no warning that it was there, no gradual sloping that would have prepared him for it. One moment he was walking on level ground and the next he had broken through some bushes, toppled over the unseen edge, and was zipping down the nearly vertical bank. He threw out his hands and tried to dig his fingers into the dirt. He jerked out a hurried "Look out!" to warn Jaybird. His stomach fluttered in the curious feeling that comes with an unexpected fall and his outstretched fingers tingled. But it was his feet that first felt the shock of the abrupt landing. It was not a very violent shock and Augustus looked up and saw the top of the bank about six feet above him. His warning had stopped Jaybird in time and Augustus saw him peering over the edge looking down. In front of Augustus the faint moonlight showed a narrow rutted clay road with a bank on the opposite side similar to the one Augustus had fallen down.

Jaybird eased himself down the slope and said, "It's the old Waymanville Road. I knew it was here but I forgot to tell you."

Augustus snorted. He had an uneasy feeling that his

fall had not been very dignified and hadn't put his abilities as a scout in a very good light.

"Huh," he grumbled, "what kind of an ol' road is this, sinkin' down into the ground like a blame ol' ditch where it don't belong?"

Jaybird grinned. "All these little ol' country roads are sunk like this in some places," he announced.

Augustus walked out on the road. It wasn't much of a road, just a cut in the red clay hillside. Apparently it wasn't traveled much, but there were two ruts in the loose clay. Augustus bent and ran his fingers along the bottom of a rut. He felt the marks of a tire tread. He straightened and looked up the road again. The pipe-line clearing was up that way. Augustus snapped his fingers.

"I guess they got away," he said. "I bet they came up this road in a car an' got out up there where the road runs near the pipe line. Then when they ran away, they just got into their car and drove off."

It sounded sensible and Jaybird agreed. "Well, nothin' much we can do now," he said. "We might as well go down to the camp an' tell 'em what happened.

"Yeh," said Augustus sadly, "but let's go on up the road a way. Maybe we can see where they parked the car." His voice brightened. "Maybe they dropped something and we might find it, some sort of clue like detectives always find. That's the way they get who they're after."

"Huh," said Jaybird as they walked up the road. "Too bad they got away. I reckon they'd be sorry if we caught up with 'em."

Augustus said, "Yeh, I guess we'd fix 'em. Boy, those ol' spies wouldn't ever know what hit 'em if we'd only found 'em."

"Spies," said Jaybird scornfully. "This is the way I'd do to 'em." He clenched his fists and swung both arms fiercely, ending with a kick so hard that he nearly lost his balance.

"Yeh," said Augustus. "This is how I'd do." He leaped ahead and grabbed the neck of an imaginary spy, choked and shook him for a while, making horrible noises to indicate the spy's unhappy state, and then threw him easily over the tree-tops. "I guess that'd fix him," he concluded, slapping his hands together to remove the dust of the brief encounter.

"Yeh," said Jaybird.

"An' that's only just the beginning of how I'd do." Augustus added, "Now look, just suppose there was an' ol' spy up the road there. This is how I'd do to him." He ran up the road waving both arms.

Jaybird ran to catch up with him but Augustus stopped so suddenly that Jaybird hit him with a bump that sent them both sprawling. Jaybird had started to get up when Augustus grabbed his arm.

"Shh," Augustus hissed. "Th—th—there's s—something there."

They lay on the road and peered ahead. Then Jaybird saw what Augustus had seen, the glitter of moonlight reflected from glass or shiny metal. The road was no longer sunk below high banks. Here it was level with the ground on both sides and the glittering thing was behind the high

bushes that marked the edge of the woods on the right side.

Augustus and Jaybird had the same idea at the same time. They wriggled across the road and crawled into the bushes on the left side of the road.

"It—it looks like a car," Jaybird whispered.

"It *is* a car." Augustus squinted through the bushes. "I betcha it's *their* car."

He and Jaybird lay silently for a while watching.

"I don't see anyone," Augustus whispered finally. He rose to his knees. "I don't hear anyone." He stood up and stared across the road. "I'm going to find out," he said, and dropping to his hands and knees he crawled across the road and into the bushes on the other side. Jaybird followed.

They crept through the bushes, stopping every few steps to look and listen. The car was well hidden from the road but when Augustus circled and stood on the slope above it he could see it clearly. It stood in the nearly dried-up bed of a stream where a small trickle of water crossed the road and wandered off through the woods. There was no sign of anyone near.

Augustus cautiously crept closer. Still he could see no one. He went on. There was no one in the car. Augustus went up and walked around it. The trunk in the back was open. A burlap bag lay on the ground below the open trunk. Augustus put his hand into the bag. "Wax," he said. "That proves it's their car. Guess one of 'em forgot this bag."

"But why didn't they come back here and drive away?" Jaybird asked.

"Dunno." Augustus shrugged. "I guess maybe when those hornets lit into 'em they just took off without worrying about which way they were going." He giggled a little. "They didn't know what was goin' on an' they prob'ly were scared to come back here."

"Mm." Jaybird's voice was serious. "They'll get over that. They'll come back for their car."

Augustus nodded. "Uh-huh," he said.

"An' that means we'd better look out or they'll catch us here," Jaybird went on.

"Uh-huh," said Augustus again, "but it means something else too."

"What?"

Augustus' voice shook a little but more from excitement than fright as he answered, "It means we'll have another chance to catch *them*."

CHAPTER TWELVE

Augustus said, "The first thing to do is fix it so's they can't get away."

Jaybird didn't think that was as simple as the tone of Augustus' voice suggested. He found it hard to think and at the same time listen for sounds that would mean the men were coming back to their car.

"We could let the air out of their tires," he suggested.

Augustus considered that. "An' we could pull all the wires out of the engine," he added. Even as he said it he saw what was wrong with both those plans.

"The trouble is," he said, "those things would keep 'em from getting away in the car, but that wouldn't stop 'em from just walking off." He scowled at the car and kicked one of the tires. "An' if they get away this time, maybe no one would ever find them."

Jaybird said, "Maybe what we need is a secret weapon." He looked at the trees as if hoping to see another hornets' nest.

Augustus repeated, "Secret weapon," and he too looked around for something that might suggest a new development in secret weapons.

"I expect they'll be comin' back pretty soon," Jaybird said uneasily.

Augustus stared down the dim aisles between the trees. The thought of the men's return was like a weight pressing on him, interfering with his breathing and squeezing his mind dry of schemes to meet the situation.

The little night noises of the woods startled him. There was something evil and ghostlike about even the creek bed. The water had worn down through the red clay and exposed a layer of white clay underneath. Augustus knew what it was. He had seen the same thing often since he came to Georgia, but tonight the white outline of the stream bed seemed to wriggle out of the woods toward him like a great pale snake.

Augustus felt a prickling on the back of his neck as his mind insisted on adding to the real dangers that confronted him. He tried to look away from the dimly white form but his eyes returned to it again and again. He shook himself angrily and told himself, "Shucks, it's just an ol' stream an' anyway it doesn't look like anything else except maybe a trail twistin' through the woods." Something in his mind clung to those words, "Like a trail—like a trail twisting through the woods." A trail was something you followed to get somewhere or . . . Augustus' mouth popped open—a trail was also something you followed if you were chasing someone who had gone down that trail.

Augustus knew his mind was ticking away toward a big idea. He recognized the feeling. It was the same as a glow of warmth after being cold. He pushed his thoughts harder.

The creek bed was like a trail because it was white against the dark red of the clay around it. That white would show anywhere against the red clay of these Georgia hills. It would be easily seen against the red clay of the road.

Augustus knew now he had the idea he needed. If he could get the spies to leave a trail as they drove away . . . But how could he accomplish that? Then he knew and was not at all happy over his knowledge. He would have to go with the spies and make the trail himself, while Jaybird went to the camp to get soldiers to follow it. Augustus thought of the open trunk in the back of the car. He could hide in there. He shivered as he thought of it but as he shivered he knew this was the big chance he had been hoping for, his chance to help the Army.

"Come on," he said to Jaybird. "We have to hurry. They'll be back any time now."

Jaybird thought he could feel his hair curl as he listened to Augustus explain his plan. "But . . . but . . ." he blurted. "Suppose they find you?"

Augustus was sure he could feel his hair curl as he considered that possibility. He didn't answer Jaybird directly, but what he said implied his answer. "Hurry up. Help me lift this sack."

They carried the big sack of wax to a thick clump of bushes and dumped it in the blackest shadows.

Then with sticks they dug out enough of the white clay to fill the big sack. Filled with clay, the sack was much heavier than when the wax was in it. Augustus and Jaybird found they could barely lift it and had to drag it to the car. There, with a final desperate heave, they got it up and into the trunk. They were working fast now, spurred by the thought that the men would surely be back for the car soon.

"Now you beat it," Augustus said. "Get down to the camp as fast as you can. Tell them what happened and get them to come up here and follow the trail I'll leave."

"Maybe the soldiers will get here in time to catch them before they start," said Jaybird hopefully.

"Yeh—if you hurry," said Augustus, but he had a feeling that this was not very likely.

Jaybird started off. "I know a man that lives down this road a way," he said over his shoulder. "Mr. Jackson—he's got a car and I'll get him to carry me to the camp. It won't take long."

He was gone. Augustus heard a rustle as he went through the bushes and then the pound of his feet getting fainter and fainter down the road.

Augustus looked around quickly to see if he had forgotten anything. It occurred to him that he would have to hold the trunk door open a little to dribble his white clay trail onto the red road. He cut a stick and jammed it between the door lock and the floor of the car. That left enough of an opening. He'd have to hold the door against the stick so it wouldn't rattle, though. There was no handle inside the door, but he decided he could hold it by the lock and a bar which made a good handhold.

"That'll be all right," he decided.

He was feeling very well satisfied with himself for thinking of everything when this pleasant feeling was smashed by a horrible thought. It came as he stood looking at the car. It was a big car, with long flowing lines that indicated speed. What if it was fast enough to get away from the cars at the camp? Augustus wrapped his arms around himself as if a sudden chill had struck him. His imagination had no trouble in thinking up what would happen to him if the spies got away and he was found hiding in the car.

He seemed to hear a quivery little voice say, "Well, you don't have to go."

He shook his head to drive the voice away but it returned. He twisted his face into a scowl in an effort to think of something else. He tried to reason it out. The danger was that the enemy's car might get away. Therefore the thing to do was . . .

Augustus stopped short and grunted aloud at the simplicity of the answer that had come to him. The noise he made surprised him and reminded him that he must be quiet. He looked around uneasily and then darted a little way into the woods where he stooped and groped for something on the ground.

When he came back he was grinning despite a curious tendency toward shakiness which his knees had developed. He fumbled at the back of the car for a minute and then after a last look around he crawled into the trunk and lowered the door against the stick he had braced to hold it open a few inches.

CHAPTER THIRTEEN

He didn't know when the men came. One minute they were not there and the next, there they were, standing beside the car talking in hurried low tones.

"What I say is, get out of here quick."

"And not finish that job with the pipe line?"

"Listen, I tell you we didn't step on that hornets' nest. I saw something fly through the air just before they started in on us. Someone threw that hornets' nest and by this time they've probably got the whole Army up there waiting for us to come back."

"You're crazy. Who'd pick up a hornets' nest and throw it? Besides——"

"I don't care. There's something wrong and I'm pulling out of here right now."

It was the Jap who wanted to stay. But the others would not be persuaded. The car doors opened and slammed shut. The starter whined. Augustus felt the vibration of the motor shake the floor under him. The big car lurched as the wheels spun and then grabbed in the slippery clay. Augustus' hiding place was filled with a pounding rumble and he clutched frantically at the lock to keep the door from thumping and banging. Holding the door took all of his attention as the car rolled and bucked over the uneven ground.

It stopped, backed and went ahead again as the driver turned and twisted between trees to head toward the road. An occasional splash of water against the mudguards beside Augustus told him they had turned back into the stream bed. Then came a lurch that almost tore the door from his fingers, and then the car steadied and gained speed. Augustus knew they were on the road now, and reaching into the sack and crumbling a clod of white clay, he dribbled it through his fingers and out the narrow opening below the door.

"Have to watch for turns and forks mostly," he thought. "As long as we stick to a straight road we'll be easy to follow."

He lay with his face pressed against the floor looking out through the narrow opening. Whenever the road widened into what might have been a fork, or when they came to a crossroad, he dropped an extra quantity of clay.

As the car picked up speed he found it impossible to be sure about forks. He knew that if he left a continuous trail the clay would not last very long. It was hard to decide what to do. If he ran out of clay before the cars from the camp picked up the trail and got close enough to see the fleeing car . . . That would be bad. Would it be as bad as to save his clay and take a chance on holding up the pursuers while they checked up on every little fork and lane?

Augustus decided it was better to be doing something

even if it was the wrong thing and he dropped his white trail in an almost continuous line except when high banks on both sides showed that there could be no other roads branching off.

His position was cramped and uncomfortable. The floor was hard and had not been designed as a pleasant place to lie on for a fast ride over rough roads. It had a vicious way of rising with a jerk and crashing into Augustus' chin or cheekbone. He hadn't gone far when these and various other ex-

posed parts were bruised and sore. Twice as he was turning his head the floor rose and smacked the bony ridges under his eyes and Augustus knew he would have two black eyes to remember his ride by. He hoped that would be the worst of the things he would remember. If the cars from the camp didn't pick up the trail . . . In that case he probably wouldn't remember anything. But the worst thought of all was knowing that the enemy rode in comfort on the soft seats over his head, while he took a pounding on the hard floor.

"Just wait!" he thought. "Just you wait. I'll show you."

The sack that held the white clay grew flat and limp with only a small bulge in one corner where a few last clods of clay remained.

Augustus' exploring fingers gauged the size of the remnants and he realized that he wasn't showing anyone anything except, perhaps, that he was showing himself that his plan might fail.

There was no chance now for him to leave a continuous trail. He would have to hoard his scraps, using them only when he was sure branching roads made marking absolutely necessary. He pressed his face close to the small opening and watched the road spin away. Twisting his neck he turned his ear to the opening, thrust it closer, held it there rigidly as a thrill of hope flashed through him.

It was a far-off sound he heard. Always faint with distance, it sometimes died away altogether. Augustus closed his eyes and hunched up his shoulders in an effort to put all his strength into listening. The sound came again and this time it seemed a little stronger. Now Augustus was sure that it wasn't just his imagination; sure, too, that the throbbing hum could be only the noise of speeding motors.

Breathless, he turned his head to bring his eyes to the opening as the car reached the top of a long rise and started down. For an instant, as the rear wheels swung over the ridge, Augustus could see far down the road as it stretched away into the valley behind. And swinging into the valley, two tiny shafts of light raced through the night. Then two more followed. That would mean four headlights. Two cars going at such a speed on this lonely road could mean only one thing. Now the final test would come.

Augustus heard an excited buzz of talk over his head and knew the spies had seen the other cars. Augustus had thought he was going fast before, but now the floor seemed to jump away from under him and a tickling sensation raced through him as the car leaped ahead at a speed that seemed like something in a dream. Augustus hung on grimly and stared back for another glimpse of the following lights. He caught one faint gleam and then no more.

"They're falling back." Augustus said it aloud and didn't much care if the men above him heard. If the Army cars couldn't overtake them he'd be found sooner or later anyway.

The car roared on, swaying and jouncing dangerously. It swung sharply to the right. Augustus saw the road they had been following swerve off and continue on its course. The bouncing of the car indicated they had turned into an even rougher road.

Augustus knew it was time to drop some white clay to mark the turn. He had just two clods left. He crumbled one and dropped the pieces, wondering if it was worth while. What good would it do if the Army cars couldn't catch them? he asked himself.

And then he remembered, remembered that he had done something to take care of just this possibility. Maybe there was still a chance. Would his trick work? He watched anxiously for pursuing headlights and listened for the sound of motors. And now he listened, too, to the roaring motor of the car he was in. Was it just his imagination or was there a slight break in the powerful growling rhythm?

He saw a thin flicker of light, far back. The Army cars had not been lost, had not given up the chase.

Now the skip in the spies' motor was so clear that it could not be mistaken. Augustus heard anxious, shouted questions. The skip grew to a steady sputter. The motor seemed choked. Augustus felt a jerk and then a sharp high whine as the driver shifted gears. The whine rose to a scream. Even in the lower gear the motor faltered.

Then came the smooth gliding motion that meant the car was coasting with the clutch disengaged. The motor raced in a series of sharp blasts. Augustus thought that was intended to blow out anything that might be blocking the flow of gas. Augustus thought, too, that it wouldn't work. He had a good reason for thinking that.

Glaring lights swung around a curve behind. The whir of the wheels under Augustus had grown slower and slower. The motor sound was now a feeble coughing. Then there was no sound at all. The forward motion died away altogether as the lights behind swept up in a blinding glare that bored into Augustus' cramped hiding place.

Augustus swung the door of the trunk up and scrambled out into the light.

"Get 'em!" he yelled. "Catch 'em! Hold 'em! Don't let 'em get away!"

He had a blurred sense of men piling out of the car back of him and dashing across an open field beside the road.

"There they go!" he yelled, but the other cars had already started. They swept past Augustus, bucked across a ditch, crashed through the bushes that lined the road and dived across the field.

"Good ol' jeeps!" yelled Augustus admiringly as he recognized the outlines of the little cars filled with soldiers. A shot barked, and another. Then the louder crash of several shots together. Silence. Out in the field the lights of the two cars met on three men who stood with their arms raised.

Following an order, they got into the jeeps which snorted back to the road and stopped beside Augustus and the stalled car.

A small figure jumped from one of the jeeps and yelled, "There he is! There he is!" It was Jaybird.

Augustus found himself in the center of a ring of soldiers. An officer was asking questions. Augustus showed him how he had hidden in the trunk and how he had left the trail of white clay. The officer looked into the burlap bag.

He said, "You were just about out of that clay and we'd

have lost them sure after you ran out and couldn't mark the trail." He slapped Augustus' shoulder. "Boy, it's mighty lucky for all of us that their car broke down."

"Lucky?" asked Augustus, grinning happily. "That wasn't luck. I fixed that up myself."

The officer stared at him. "You—you what?"

"Yeh," said Augustus, "I fixed it. I kind of figured they might get away, so I just dumped some of their own wax into their gas tank—you know, the wax they were putting in the pipe line to spoil the gas at the camp."

The officer didn't say anything for a long time. He shook his head. Then he shook hands with Augustus very seriously. "Come on," he said. "We'll take you kids home. Then we'll put these spies where they belong." He laughed. "And then I'll tell the General what you did and you'll probably get a medal. You ought to."

The jeep's lights shone on the front of the tent where Augustus lived. The picture of the fat lady and the sign SAVE THE FAT AND WIN THE WAR stood out sharply in the bright light.

Pop, Ma, Glorianna and Jupiter stood beside the entrance. They all rushed up when Augustus and Jaybird climbed down from the jeep.

"Oh, land's sakes," said Ma nervously, "are you arrested? What did you do? I declare to the everlasting mountains I never did see such a young'un."

The officer said, "No, lady, they're not arrested. They're probably going to get a medal for helping the Army."

Ma blinked. Augustus grinned at her and at Pop.

"Sure," he said. "I told you I was going to help the Army, so I just did."

"Well, fry both my feet for a couple of catfish!" Pop bellowed. "I always did say he takes after my side of the family."

"Sakes alive!" snorted Ma, but she was too busy being proud of Augustus even to argue with Pop.

Augustus and Jaybird grinned at each other, and Augustus said, "Well, I guess we showed 'em!"